THE GILDED KISS

It was the key to a most baffling exploit for Dale Shand, but a lot was to happen to him and the bewitching Linda Travers before he found it. For her, Shand leaves his new headquarters in Baker Street, London, to travel across Europe and back, where he follows a trail of murder and big-time art theft. In a high-octane adventure, he encounters a sinister Spaniard, a mysterious girl and a missing heir — all enmeshed in the tangled web.

Books by Douglas Enefer
in the Linford Mystery Library:

THE DEADLY STREAK
THE LAST LEAP
THE SIXTH RAID
LAKESIDE ZERO
ICE IN THE SUN
THE DEADLINE DOLLY
A LONG WAY TO PITT STREET
THE GIRL CHASE

DOUGLAS ENEFER

◆

THE GILDED KISS

Complete and Unabridged

LINFORD
Leicester

First published in Great Britain by
Robert Hale Limited, London

First Linford Edition
published 2006
by arrangement with
Robert Hale Limited, London

British Library CIP Data

Enefer, Douglas
    The gilded kiss.—Large print ed.—
    Linford mystery library
    1. Detective and mystery stories
    2. Large type books
    I. Title
    823.9′14 [F]

    ISBN 1–84617–417–1

Published by
F. A. Thorpe (Publishing)
Anstey, Leicestershire

Set by Words & Graphics Ltd.
Anstey, Leicestershire
Printed and bound in Great Britain by
T. J. International Ltd., Padstow, Cornwall

This book is printed on acid-free paper

To

Ted and Wyn Dickinson

1

Nancy looked up from her neat desk and announced: 'A phone call for you — from New York.' Her voice made the simple statement sound as if the call was coming from extragalactic space.

It almost was. Two months previously I had opened a London office in Baker Street; if the address was good enough for Sherlock Holmes it would do for Dale Shand.

I had been thinking of making the move for some time, but it was old Josiah Ballinger Halcyon who had finally clinched it by recommending me to a British industrial consortium who wanted both the consultative and periodically active services of a private investigator of outstanding credentials, personal appearance and known sobriety. According to J.B., I tested high in all these criteria, a thing I wouldn't have claimed for myself. He was prejudiced, anyway.

Some time before, he had hired me on an assignment which took me to England — a country I first became fond of nearly two decades ago when I saw it with the U.S. Army. I managed to report enough success to pick up a twenty thousand dollar bonus and the promise of lucrative top-level introductions. It was the British one which had persuaded me to open a branch in London, and Nancy had come over with me — at last realizing her girlish dream of becoming personal secretary and ally-in-chief to Dale Shand. Well, off and on she had served a kind of apprenticeship while supervising the telephone switchboard at the quiet midtown apartment block in New York where I had had my home since arriving in Manhattan from the Middle West full of the bitter-sweet pangs and resolutions of youth.

Once we had almost been close, but I had shied off. I knew that with Nancy it would have to be marriage and I was thirty-eight at the time and getting set in my habits, which is perhaps no more than a way of saying I'm too self-centred to make a good husband.

There *is* another factor, though. Much of the work I do is uneventful to the point of being dull, but every once in a while it explodes in violence. When that happens I live with the knowledge that I could walk out some dark night and never come back, except in an ambulance heading for the morgue slab in The Tombs, and I won't ask a wife to share that anxiety. Maybe private investigating in England wouldn't present the same hazards, in which case I might still ask Nancy to become Mrs. Dale Shand.

But not just yet . . .

I glanced down at her as I walked across to take the call. She looked the way she always looks — as if she had just taken a shower and shampoo and put herself into her neatest white blouse and dark skirt. You'll *have* to marry her some time, Shand, or you'll lose her to some enterprising Englishman.

'The caller is Mr. Jesse Melford Leffiney with an address in the East Seventies,' intoned Nancy.

'What — the old coot who made an

indecently large pile back in the Roaring Twenties?'

Nancy nodded, her dark brown hair glinting under the fluorescent lighting. 'Yes, Mr. Shand — though I doubt if he would care to hear himself described precisely in those terms.'

I grinned. 'You had a hand over the mouthpiece, didn't you?'

'Yes, I think of everything,' said Nancy calmly.

I took the receiver from her and said: 'Shand here. Good afternoon, Mr. Leffiney, though it's still morning where you are. What can I do for you?'

'I have a commission I wish you to handle.' The voice had a sort of rasping edge to it, as if he had grit in his mouth; but it wasn't the voice of a very old man, though he was that all right — pushing ninety, if my arithmetic was correct.

I said: 'Look, Mr. Leffiney, I'm working out of London for some time to come . . . '

'I thought you commuted between there and New York, young man.'

'Occasionally, but right now I'm not

free to do it. I have a major investigation coming up within the next two weeks.'

'Excellent, Shand — it means you're free just at the right moment.'

'Not entirely. I've a conference lined up. And, in any event, I can't leave London in case . . . '

'I'm not *asking* you to leave London, young man,' he snapped.

'I like this reiterated stuff about my being young, Mr. Leffiney.'

'To a man of my age you're scarcely out of diapers,' the rasping voice said. 'Specifically, I can give you exactly forty-nine years, eleven months, two weeks and a day.'

'So you've been looking me up?'

'In more ways than that. I like to know a few basic things about any man I hire.'

'You haven't hired me yet and I haven't yet decided that you're going to, Mr. Leffiney.'

'Your operating rate and normal expenses, plus a five thousand dollar bonus for a task which need occupy you no more than a few days, if that.'

'I told you I can't leave England . . . '

'Don't keep interrupting, God damn you. The assignment *is* in England.'

'I'm interested, Mr. Leffiney.'

The rasp modulated into a dry chuckle. 'I thought you might be. My researches indicate that a desire for money is one of your virtues.'

'Some people regard it as a vice.'

'Then they're fools. Money means power.'

'I don't care much about that . . . '

'Independence, then. I hear you set considerable store on independence — even to the extent of exercising it when you haven't actually got it.'

'Talking of money,' I said thoughtfully, 'this call is costing you the earth and we haven't even got down to details.'

'At the last count I was reckoned to be worth twenty-two million, not including the current value of my penthouse in New York and that damned great mausoleum of a house down in Virginia that I'm still sentimental enough to keep.'

'Nice work if you can get it,' I said drily.

'I've got it,' said Jesse Melford Leffiney,

'and I didn't get it by extravagance, nor do I place this telephone call in that category.'

'You could have written to me. Much cheaper.'

'I prefer at all times to do business in person, and in your absence from New York the telephone is the next best thing. I want you to go down to a place called Thetford in Norfolk and find out if anyone named Leffiney lives there.'

'That's your name. I didn't know you had a branch of the family over here.'

'Neither did I until three weeks ago. I knew we came over to America from England, probably some years before the war of the States, but my father never said where and as both he and my mother died when I was still at college I didn't have anyone to ask — even supposing I was interested, which I wasn't. For the next forty years I was too busy getting ahead.'

'What happened three weeks ago, Mr. Leffiney?' I asked patiently; patience was a virtue I could afford in this conversation.

'I received a letter from a man in Philadelphia, a man named Adelberger — Peter Adelberger. I have never heard of him, but he said that on a recent visit to England he encountered the name Leffiney in Norfolk and wondered if they were connected with the Leffineys over here, of whom I am the sole survivor.'

'What's *his* interest?'

'None, in a personal sense. It turns out that he does some business with an export company in which I still have an interest, knew my name and was struck by the coincidence, particularly as the name is unusual.'

'What do you want me to do — just find somebody named Leffiney in Norfolk and report back?'

'Correct.'

'The name may be no more than coincidence.'

'I haven't finished yet, Shand. I called in a firm which specializes in tracing family ancestries. They came up with the information that a family named Leffiney emigrated from this part of Norfolk in 1859, settling in Virginia — where I was

8

born. The connection is thus specific and conclusive.'

'You could check out the English roots of your family tree through Somerset House — or get another specialist firm in England to do it. There are several over here doing that kind of work.'

'I am not interested in the detailed ramifications of the English connection, not at this stage. I want a reliable representative to go there — in person. You fit.'

'You don't even know me.'

Another dry chuckle travelled three thousand costly miles. 'I've had *you* checked out pretty thoroughly — from the District Attorney to Josiah Ballinger Halcyon. Any man who impresses J.B. is likely to meet my requirements.'

I looked at my watch. The bill for this call was now assuming tycoon proportions. I said: 'This guy Adelberger — didn't *he* meet anybody of your name while he was here?'

'He didn't have time. He was motoring through the territory on the way back to London. He was due to fly home that night. He simply heard the name in some hotel and made a note to mention it to me. I was sufficiently interested to have inquires made as to whether my father did in fact come from Norfolk.'

'Are you doing all this out of interest in the family origins or is there another reason?'

'You're thinking acutely, Shand. I like that. There *is* a specific reason. The date of my death cannot, in the nature of things, be long postponed. I have no widow, no children. I shall die an immensely rich man.'

'Somebody in Norfolk is going to be lucky, Mr. Leffiney.'

'*If* he is in the direct line. And if I like him — or her.'

'You want me to *bring* them to America?'

'In due course. Not immediately. First I want your factual report and your personal impressions.' The voice took on the rasping edge again. 'Time is money, Shand — get moving.'

I put the phone down. Nancy had been listening on the extension. I never take a case nowadays without her being in the picture. If I don't watch out I'll become a cipher in my own office.

'A somewhat odd assignment, Mr. Shand.' She was tapping her small teeth with the blunt end of a beautifully sharpened pencil. All Nancy's pencils are beautifully sharpened, like her wits.

'Simple, though.'

'Just a pleasant drive up to Norfolk, a good hotel, a few inquiries round the area, salary £35 a day plus expenses, plus a five thousand dollar bonus for a satisfactory completion.'

'Like finding money by the wayside, you mean?'

'Not really. Your present success is the end product of all those years of struggling.'

'Yeah — three weeks sitting alone in a musty office, smoking too many cigarettes and waiting for the clients who don't show. I've had all that.'

Nancy gave me her quick warm smile, both with her mouth and her eyes, then as quickly ended it. 'I wish you wouldn't say yeah for yes. It has a sort of common sound.'

11

'Well, I'm a sort of common man.'

'No, you're not. You sometimes like to make people think you're common and tough and cynical, but you're not any of those things. You're . . . never mind,' said Nancy primly.

'Book me into a nice olde world hotel in Thetford,' I said. 'One with a nice olde world bar.'

'Tck!' said Nancy. But she did it. When she put the phone down she said: 'If Mr. Kenning phones what do I tell him?' Jack Kenning was the managing director of the industrial outfit currently paying me a considerable retainer.

'The truth, it's always best. I've had to go up to Norfolk — or is it down? He can ring me at the hotel there.'

'Right.' She ringed the number she had noted on a scratch-pad, tore the sheet off and put it in a folder already marked *Leffiney Case*. Then she looked up and said: 'How do you like it here in England?'

'I like it swell, Nancy. And you?'

'It's a wonderful world, as your favourite musician said a while back.'

12

'Louis Armstrong?'

'Of course.'

'Greatest jazzman who ever lived. There won't be anyone like him in the next hundred years. Put a call through to Philadelphia, will you?'

Nancy's eyes jumped. 'The *cost!*' she gasped.

'We'll put it on the Leffiney account. Contact Tod Burling of the Cohn-Burling Agency and have him come through with a rundown on Peter Adelberger.'

'You don't mean you suspect him of making the whole thing up, do you?' asked Nancy in alarm.

'I don't mean anything — I just like to have the background filled in on any case I'm going to handle. I'll be back in an hour — got to pack.'

'I have our emergency suitcase permanently packed,' said Nancy.

'That's fine — it'll give me time to have the car washed and checked over. See you, then.'

I went out aware that she was following me with her eyes and wondering if I was lying. I was — at least in the sense that I could have the car checked while I joined Freddie Stanway in the Fleet Street pub he was likely to be visiting in less than thirty-five minutes from now, which would make it opening time.

When I got back Nancy said, a trifle coldly I thought: 'Car in order, Mr. Shand?'

'Yeah — I mean yes.'

'Did you enjoy your drink?'

'I'll have to start using those little drops that neutralize the aroma.'

'I'd still know,' said Nancy. 'By the way, Tod Burling's been on the wire.'

'What, already?'

'Yes. He says there's nobody named Adelberger at the Philadelphia address you gave me.'

'Oh? Well, maybe the guy's moved his apartment.'

'That would be a tenable theory except for one thing . . . '

'Oh — what's that?'

'*There's no such address*,' said Nancy.

2

I went north out of London, driving a year-old Hillman Minx which I bought when I started up in England — partly because I liked the car anyway and subconsciously perhaps because it reminded me of a girl I had known here last summer. She was married now to Jimmy Halcyon, who would inherit old J.B.'s money one of these days.

I checked-in at the hotel Nancy had fixed, freshened up with a shower, a second shave and a change of clothes and went down into the bar. The fellow behind the counter, a jovial soul with handlebar moustaches and a neat imperial beard, seemed to be gifted with psychic powers. Before my elbows had touched wood he said richly: 'Scotch, sir?'

'How did you guess?'

'Most American gentlemen like it, sir.'

He was mixing the drink when a girl

came in and sat on the high stool next to mine.

'Evening, Miss Travers,' said the whiskered bartender.

'Hello, Joe. I'll have a bitter shandy with big dollops of ice and a slice of lemon.' Her voice was a warm contralto, not too deep. I half-turned to see her. She looked in her late twenties with an oval face framed by very dark hair, almost raven black. The face and her bare arms had a light, even suntan. She was wearing a white crocheted dress whose fashion-able mini-length hemline showed rather more leg than my old Aunt Harriet would have regarded as decorous, but my old Aunt Harriet has been long gone.

Joe said: 'This gentleman is over here from America.'

The girl, who had reached for her glass, put it down abruptly. 'Oh?' she said. Suddenly, the mellow voice had a small brittle edge to it.

'Yes. My name is Shand — Dale Shand.'

She picked up her glass again without immediately drinking from it. 'I suppose you're over here sight-seeing?' she ventured.

I thought I was seeing one of the more agreeable sights of the locality, but I didn't mention it. Instead, I said: 'Not in the ordinary way. I'm living in England. Just down here on some business.'

'Oh?' she said again. Then, quite suddenly, she smiled. 'That's a coincidence. *I'm* here on business, too. Linda Travers is the name.' She held out a cool, slim hand. 'Nice to know you, Mr. Shand. An American living in England, are you?'

'In London. I've been here several months.'

'You're not a newspaperman, by any chance?'

'I used to be. It was rather a long time ago, though. In New York. Why, what makes you ask?'

She laughed, and the edginess might never have been in her voice. 'I'm in the trade myself — the magazine field. I just wondered if you were.'

'Miss Travers is down here writing some articles about this part of Norfolk,' offered Joe.

I lit a pipe and said: 'Then you may be able to give me some information, Miss Travers. I'm looking for one or more members of a family believed to originate here, name of Leffiney.'

She shook her head. 'No, I don't believe I know that name.'

'You must mean old Ben Leffiney,' said Joe. 'Lives out at Oak Hall Farm. It's on the forest road about half-way to Brandon.'

'Well, thanks. I seem to have come to the right place for information — I was half expecting to find there wasn't anyone of that name around here.'

'Used to be a number of them, sir. But now there's only old Ben left. Well, he's only about fifty — but everybody calls him old Ben.'

I suddenly became aware that Linda Travers was looking sideways at me. Then she said: 'Why, are you interested in old county families, Mr. Shand?'

'Not specially. Just the Leffiney family.'

'I see.' She toyed absently with her shandy and went on: 'Quite a number of big families here — what's left of the old landed gentry.'

'I guess there are, Miss Travers.'

'Well, there's more of them than you might think. All the stately homes of England haven't yet become vacant under the burden of taxation or been taken over by the National Trust.'

'That's swell.'

'You're just saying that,' she accused. 'I'll bet you don't even care.'

'Because I'm a damned Yank?'

She coloured faintly. 'I wasn't trying to be rude, Mr. Shand.'

'That's all right. As a matter of fact, Americans are supposed to be even more interested in the stately homes than the British themselves.'

'Oh — are *you*?' Again there was a small hardness in her voice.

'I hadn't really thought about it, I was just looking for this Leffiney connection.'

'Yes, so you said.'

'Ben used to come in here regularly,' mused Joe. 'I haven't seen him lately, though. But there's been a bit of a virus going round and he may have caught the bug for all I know.' The bartender chuckled. 'Must have done, come to think

19

of it, or he'd have been in. Likes his wallop, does old Ben.'

Linda Travers said: 'It sounds inquisitive, but what makes you interested in him?'

I hesitated, but there didn't seem to be any reason for not telling her. 'Well, I may be able to bring him a piece of news. He could be the heir to a fortune.'

'Really?' The way she spoke the word sounded almost derisive. I was starting to feel irritated by this otherwise attractive girl.

Joe the bartender, on the other hand, was all ears. They were almost flapping like a couple of flags. 'You don't say?'

'A very rich old man in New York who has the same name thinks his sole surviving heir may be living around here and asked me to make some inquiries.'

'Well, well!' said Miss Linda Travers.

'What's that mean?' I was getting needled.

'Nothing, except that it's a gorgeous story.'

'You could put it in one of your articles if it turns out that old Ben *is* an heir, Miss

Travers,' said Joe.

'So I could — *if* it stands up.' She snapped open her handbag, took a filter-tipped cigarette from a small white calfskin case and lit it.

More customers drifted in and Joe moved off down the bar. I made my mind up. 'Look, Miss Travers, I may have got this all wrong — but I have an idea you don't believe me.'

'Well, really — why on earth shouldn't I?'

'I'm damned if I know, but that's the impression I'm getting.'

'You're letting your imagination run away with you, Mr. Shand.'

'I don't think so. But if I am, I apologize.' I held another lighted match over the bowl of my pipe and added: 'I didn't make up that name, you know. There *is* a Ben Leffiney living round here.'

'So it seems. Perhaps *I* ought to do the apologizing.'

'What for?'

'My manner, which is apparently annoying you, Mr. Shand.'

'Yeah, it is — or was. You sound rather nicer now. What sort of articles are you doing?'

She studied the smoke wisping from her cigarette, then eyed me directly and said: 'My editor thinks there's likely to be a good deal of interest in stories dealing with family treasures — rare antiques, silver, art works and so on.'

'I guess there is, Miss Travers. I hadn't thought about it.'

'Hadn't you?' she said icily.

'For Pete's sake, what's getting into you?'

'Nothing . . . well, yes there is. I thought perhaps you might be one of those American dealers coming over here to buy up essentially English possessions — as if this country wasn't denuded enough already.'

I laughed. 'Do I *look* the part?'

'As a matter of fact, you don't — but that proves nothing.'

'I'm simply looking for Ben Leffiney . . . ' I stopped because a fellow who had seated himself down the bar suddenly got off his stool and started across the floor. He hadn't even tasted his drink. There was a book tucked under his arm and he dropped it. The book bounced close to where I sat and I reached down, picked it up and gave it back to him, getting a fast look at a tall, loosely-built man about my age with a long cadaverous face and a small puckered scar on his chin.

'Thanks,' he said. He went out into the corridor and wedged himself in a pay telephone booth.

Linda Travers slid off her stool and said: 'I must run upstairs and change. See you around, I expect.'

'I'll count the moments, Miss Travers,' I said sardonically.

'Yes, do,' she answered and was gone.

I glanced after her retreating figure, which was worth glancing at. I could also see the cadaverous man in the phone booth. He was dialling a number and staring at me with an odd expression on his face. When he caught my eye he turned, so that his back was half towards me. I put my unfinished drink down and walked out of the bar, straight up to the booth and yanked the door wide open.

He was in the middle of saying something. ' . . . yes, I told you . . . American, he's in here asking questions . . . he must be one of them . . . ' The voice, harsh as rusted wire, stopped. He slid round with the receiver held out at an angle from his body.

'I beg your pardon,' I said amiably. 'I didn't realize this booth was occupied . . . '

He didn't answer. I closed the door and went out of the hotel and round the rear for my car. I was still pondering the odd incident as I drove down the long empty road cleaving between the towering mass of the forest. The September dusk was falling, made darker by the trees and I put the headlights on full beam. The road speared straight into the distance. No houses now, nothing. But somewhere ahead was Oak Hall Farm.

The speedometer needle was nudging sixty. Better cut the speed or I might miss the place. I slowed down into the forties. I was coming out of a curve when lights suddenly blazed behind me, not just full beam but a big spotlight as well. As the road straightened again the light pierced the rear window, bounced back off the driving mirror.

The fellow must have been doing eighty. I pulled over to the left, almost into the grass verge, to let him through.

Then he was level with me, in an E-type Jaguar, all black. He was hunched down in the cockpit but I got a fleeting look at him as he went past. He wasn't wearing the face of the man in the phone booth.

He left me standing. I could see his tail lights disappearing in the distance — but they didn't completely vanish. Twin spots of red glowing strongly. He was braking.

An alarm signal gonged in my mind — without reason, without anything. But it was there.

The forest had been planted so that soft grassy clearings gave the giant trees breadth in which to live. I went off the road straight into one of them as twin bursts of orange flared from the back of the car ahead.

A high keening sound cut through the still air and was gone.

3

I didn't have a gun. Private investigators in England don't go around with one. Besides I couldn't have achieved anything even with a .38 Smith and Wesson on a .45 frame, which is considerable fire power, for the black Jag had vanished.

The keening sound had been instantly followed by a rapid succession of plops. Bullets hitting something, not me. From under the trees came a sudden crashing and a frightened deer stampeded from cover, veering diagonally across the roadway. I backed the Hillman off the soft grass and drove slowly on, trying to make any kind of sense out of what had happened, but it was too crazy. People just don't drive cars with sub-machine guns jutting out from the rear. But this fellow had. Must be some kind of a nut.

Maybe I ought to inform the local law. Later perhaps. A T-junction sign showed in the headlights. I went past the intersection and a few minutes later saw a lane on my left. At the entrance to it was a post with a carved rustic board and an arrowhead. The wording on the board said *Oak Hall Farm*.

I turned into the lane and drove along it about fifty yards and found the place. Whoever named it a hall must have had a whimsical sense of humour because it was no more than a moderately roomy house, an old half-timbered house with a sloping thatched roof needing attention. The black and white double gates were open on a dirt drive which wound along the side of the place. A car stood on the drive, a spattered Austin Cambridge with rust pimples on the fender.

Light showed from behind curtained windows. I walked up a short, flagged path and dragged on a bellrope. Cracked chimes started up somewhere inside. They faded, heavy footsteps sounded and the door opened and I was seeing a tall man in a soiled Harris tweed jacket with dark brown leather stitched on the elbows and cuffs. He wore a check shirt which bulged above a cracked leather belt holding up crumpled cord slacks. His face was square and tanned and the thick hair, growing to a point above the broad forehead, was wholly grey. Yet in an odd way he looked younger than his reputed years; perhaps the open-air life had given him a buoyancy denied to sedentary workers? The eyes were a light blue and curiously piercing.

'Yes?' he said.

'I take it you're Mr. Ben Leffiney,' I said.

He nodded. 'The same. What can I do for you, Mister . . . ?'

'Dale Shand. Do you mind if I come in and talk with you?'

'I ought to know something of your business first.'

'It's a somewhat long story, Mr. Leffiney — but, briefly, it could mean that you're the heir to a fortune.'

That seemed to stir him. The eyes blinked rapidly, then he chuckled. 'You're joking, of course,' he said.

'No joke, Mr. Leffiney, this is strictly on the level.' I showed him one of my cards, not the one with the crossed guns rampant.

He twitched horn-rimmed spectacles from his outside breast pocket, balanced them midway down his nose and peered at what was on the card.

'Dale Shand . . . private investigations and consultancy . . . ' He poked the card back at me and said: 'If you're a private detective what's that got to do with me inheriting a fortune?'

'Do you want me to tell you on the doorstep or would you prefer sitting down, Mr. Leffiney?'

He shrugged massive shoulders and held the door open wider. I went with him into a room with a red-tiled floor, a worn sheepskin rug, old-fashioned dark mahogany and a couple of vintage leather armchairs; pretty much the sort of room you can see in farmhouses pretty well everywhere, except that most of them now have television and he hadn't.

Ben Leffiney planted himself on the sheepskin rug, his impressive back to the vast empty fireplace.

'Well?' he said.

I told him. It took rather more than five minutes, during which he neither spoke nor moved; only his eyes betrayed mounting interest in what I was saying.

'That's it then, Mr. Leffiney,' I finished. 'Except for one thing.'

'Oh — what would that be?'

'It'll be necessary for you to produce documented proof that you are in a direct line of relationship to Jesse Melford Leffiney.'

He reached in a pocket and brought out a bent pipe and an oilskin pouch. He began filling the pipe with a sort of slow deliberateness.

'I don't know much about my antecedents,' he said. 'I didn't even know there was an American connection. I dare say the parish records will help — and then there's Somerset House.' He held a match above the pipe bowl, blew the flame out and added: 'Why didn't this Mr. Jesse Leffiney go there in the first instance?'

'He wanted someone to establish personal contact as his representative.'

'I see. Funny the whole thing should come up through a letter from a chap visiting this part of England.' He made a grin. 'Not that I'm complaining. If some long-lost second cousin or great-uncle or something wants to leave me his money I can assure you it'll be welcome.'

'Money's always welcome, Mr. Leffiney.'

'It is to me. I've had a rather difficult time lately.' He gestured with his pipe stem. 'This used to be a four hundred acre farm and profitable. I had a longish run of bad seasons and bad luck and had to sell part of it to pay off a bank loan and tax still owing from the last good year. I'm down to a hundred acres now and I farm it myself, except for one labourer who comes in.'

'You aren't married?'

'No, I never took the plunge.' A small light came in the blue eyes. 'How much is this fortune you're talking about?'

'In British currency getting on for seven million pounds.'

'Now you *must* be joking!'

I shook my head at him. For a long moment he stood there, apparently speechless. Then he said thickly: 'We'd better have a drink.'

'All right.'

He went up to the ornate mahogany sideboard, found a bottle half full of whisky and poured a couple of stiff ones.

'Good God!' he said, 'I didn't know any one man on earth had that much money.

'Well, don't count on handling it until we've established a direct relationship, Mr. Leffiney.'

He turned with his glass half-way to his mouth. 'A farmer learns not to count on anything too much, Mr. Shand. He knows that the best he can do may be brought to naught by bad weather, floods, personal illness, foot and mouth — any one of a number of factors.'

'I was just being cautious,' I said. 'The name is unusual and the old man has had his family origins traced back to this part of Norfolk. There seems little doubt that you're the last link — unless there are other Leffineys around here?'

'No, I'm the only one.'

'Then there shouldn't be any problem, Mr. Leffiney.' He gulped straight whisky and breathed out noisily. 'I can't really take it in,' he said. 'All that money . . . it seems fantastic.'

'Well, of course, it won't come your way until the old man dies, you know.'

'No . . . no, I understand that.'

'On the other hand, it's unlikely to be a long wait.'

He speared fingers through his thick grey hair. 'Ben Leffiney a millionaire . . . that'll shake a few people round these parts. My bank manager will have a fit. What's the immediate move?'

'The local parson, he'll have access to the parish records.'

'Varley — Canon John de Vere Varley, he has the living. Rector of St. Bede's. The parish church is only half a mile from here.'

'We can call on him now, if you like.'

'I'll ring him up.' Leffiney started across the room, then paused. 'Perhaps it would be better if you did it, Mr. Shand.'

'As you wish. No reason why you shouldn't come along, though.'

'I'd prefer to stay in the background — at least until it's been proved, one way or the other. Don't want to appear

33

over-anxious in front of the canon.'

'All right. I can handle it and come back later.'

He nodded and picked up the phone. When the call went through he handed the receiver to me. I told the reverend I'd appreciate calling on him on a matter of some importance and could be there within a few minutes if he could spare the time. He could.

I hung up and said: 'By the way, do you know anyone round here who owns a black E-type?'

Ben Liffiney was pouring himself another drink. He finished pouring it and said: 'No, I don't think so. I mean I don't.'

'Or a fellow with a cadaverous face and a small scar on his chin . . . '

He drank some of the whisky and shook his head. I walked out to my car and started driving. The church, which looked as if it had been there since the Normans came over, was set back from the forest road. The rectory, a rambling house with a mansard roof, looked somewhat more recent.

A maidservant with long black skirts and a starched collar to her frilled blouse showed me into the study. Less than half an hour later I had established that Benjamin Alfred Leffiney was the only son of Alfred James Leffiney, younger brother of Jesse Hardisty Leffiney, father of Jesse Melford Leffiney. The connection was specific, direct and conclusive.

Canon Varley, a solidly rotund man with a mane of sheer white hair falling off a pink dome, closed his rolltop desk and said thoughtfully: 'There are only two people in the parish, I think, who remember Alfred Leffiney. It is rather a long time ago, but there were quite a number of Leffineys here once. Well, it is a most extraordinary development. I imagine Ben Leffiney is — ah — somewhat excited.'

'As a matter of fact, he said he couldn't take it in, Canon.'

'Yes — yes, no doubt. I hope the ultimate possession of such an astronomical fortune will not be to his detriment.'

'Sometimes it is. On the other hand, he's not a very young man.'

'Older men can be foolish, Mr. Shand.

Money, particularly a great deal of unearned money, doesn't necessarily work out to human advantage.'

'I suppose not.'

'Don't misunderstand me, Mr. Shand. I am not denying that money has a place of importance or that absence of it can be humiliating, but . . . ' The stooped shoulders under the clerical black moved slightly.

I said: 'You know Ben Leffiney quite well, I imagine?'

'I thought I did.' He hesitated, then resumed: 'Ben was a member of our congregation at St. Bede's and was about to take office as a churchwarden. About a month ago, it would be, he quite abruptly and without explanation ceased to attend either Matins or Evensong.'

There didn't seem to be anything to say. I made a polite sound and he said: 'I knew Ben was having financial worries, but this seemed a poor reason for ceasing to attend church — indeed, one of the functions of religion is to offer solace in times of stress.'

'He may have become embittered or disillusioned.'

'Such a thought occurred to me, so I rang him up. He — ah — told me quite tersely that he was giving up coming to church. I reminded him that he was taking office as one of our wardens. He seemed to have completely forgotten about it.'

'Because of his money troubles?'

'I suppose so. Anyway, he withdrew his name. He seems to be living almost like a recluse.'

'I gather he farms the place himself, apart from a man who comes in.'

'Yes, Jed Harker, a rather shiftless fellow. Ben used to employ a number of men.' The rector stood up, his hands tucked in his pockets. 'Well, his financial troubles are apparently a thing of the past.'

'He can't handle any money yet.' I grinned faintly. 'Unless he can get accommodation at the bank on the strength of his expectations — which are real enough.'

'No doubt. Well, I'm happy to have

been able to help you, Mr. Shand.'

'Perhaps Ben Liffiney will return to the fold, canon, now that the end of his troubles is in sight.'

'I'd like to think so.' He accompanied me to the door and stood there until I started driving.

I was midway to the farm when I saw the black E-type again. It was off the roadway, standing on grass under the overhang of the trees, without lights. I cut my engine out, pulled the handbrake up without ratchet sound and walked carefully across the little clearing. Something stirred between the trees and there was a sudden furry movement; then the small animal was gone.

There was no other sound and I wasn't making any. I didn't approach directly, I was keeping to the line of the trees until I got close in — a lunatic who could dream-up a machine-gun gimmick for his car might have a hand automatic as well.

I came within feet of the car. Its long bonnet with the four-litre motor under it was jutting into the undergrowth, which seemed odd. I ducked low down and jumped the intervening distance. That brought me to the back of the Jag. Nothing happened. I edged round the side and saw him.

He was slumped over the wood-rimmed steering wheel, unmoving. I didn't like the way he was doing it. I didn't like anything about it. I got the door open and poked at the big neck artery.

Then I used both hands to pull at his shoulders so that I could see his face, only now he didn't have one. About half of it was a bloodied mass and he was very dead.

4

The big rangily-built man had only a slight Norfolk voice. A soft voice. There wasn't anything else soft about him. He was about an inch less than my six feet but a good deal wider — a large, compact man in a plain grey suit with a plain white shirt and a dark blue tie held in place by a gold clip. He had a broad, amiable face and a trick of shooting his shirt cuffs at intervals. Any way you looked at him, Detective Inspector John Power, C.I.D., Norfolk County Constabulary, had the general aspect of a man it would pay to get along with. I hoped we were going to.

We were in executive session at the local police station, in a room made available by Sergeant Banbury. I had called the law on Ben Leffiney's telephone and gone back to the Jag to wait. Banbury, a uniformed constable and the police doctor arrived in a Morris 1,000 with a white police band painted on it and the cowled roof light rotating. Power came under an hour later in a white Ford Zodiac with a detective sergeant, a detective constable, a photographer and a couple of lab men.

Now I was looking at John Power across a plain deal table and getting ready to tell what I had to tell for the second time and in extended detail.

He didn't seem to be in a hurry about it. A packet of twenty Players slid across the table, with an invitation to help myself. A varaflame lighter followed it. We lit up like a couple of old chums settling down for a cosy chat.

'Interesting country, America,' he said.

'Why, do you know it, inspector?'

'Went there during the war. I was in the Royal Navy — chief petty officer, then a lieutenant. A week in New York. Four days in San Francisco some time later. Had quite a time.'

'That's fine,' I said politely.

He chuckled. 'You don't care, not really. Well, why should you? You're wondering what the hell I'm nattering on about, eh? Nothing to do with the little matter in hand. Not so little, though. Tell me all about it — again.'

I sighed. 'I suppose I'll have to, inspector.'

'Tedious, going back over the same ground. Useful though, occasionally. A man can forget some minor point of detail which might be suggestive. But, of course, you'll appreciate that, being a private detective.' He didn't say it disagreeably; but, on the other hand, he didn't say it with notable enthusiasm.

'I used to be an assistant investigator in the New York District Attorney's department, inspector.'

'Better — undoubtedly better.' He eyed me genially. 'Or is it? I wonder.'

'Meaning I know the ropes?'

'Something like that. Hope it won't inhibit you from telling a full, frank and complete story, Mr. Shand.'

'It won't. Besides, the British ropes may be a little different.'

'There's that, of course. Suppose you go through it from the start, eh?'

I went through the lot — from the time the phone rang in my London office down to the moment when I found the dead man in the black E-type. Everything in — no considered or unconsidered omissions, no qualifications and no expressions of opinion. I wasn't sure whether I had any.

Power was a good listener. He was also a good interrogator — alternately deftly probing and conversationally digressing while he figured out the timing of the next question or watched your reflexes over the last one.

'What's your view, Shand?' He asked the question as if he didn't care.

'I haven't formed one yet.'

'Yet, eh? Meaning you may do later?'

'Perhaps.'

'That presupposes you'll be maintaining an active interest in the case. Not sure we'd like that.'

'It could merely mean that I may form an opinion based on what the police discover.'

He chuckled again. 'Adroitly parried, that. To use your American idiom, it doesn't necessarily buy you anything though.'

There was nothing in that for me and I let it drift on the evening breeze. Power lunged straight on. 'Bit barmy all this business of the Jag, wouldn't you say? I mean machine guns sticking out of the rear.'

'Yeah, barmy is the word.'

'Sounds like 007 and all that. Marvellous stories, those, but not within our experience — no, definitely not within our experience.'

'Until now,' I said drily.

'That's true.' He picked up a sheet of foolscap with some typed notes on it. 'Report from the brains department — how that gadget was rigged-up. Push-button control from the instrument panel. Two buttons — one for firing, one for changing the line of fire. Mirror vision, wide-angled. Clever.'

'If I hadn't swerved right off the road I'd have found it lethal.'

'Your reflexes are in excellent order, fortunately for you. Why the hell should a fellow drive round this quiet countryside or anywhere else with that kind of armoury, though — that's what I ask myself.'

44

'Do you know who he is — or was?'

'He had a driving licence in the name of James Barton Smith, of 4a Wellin Park West, Hampstead, London. Also a passport similarly made out. We've had the address checked. It exists all right. But nobody named James Barton Smith or any other kind of Smith lives there or ever has lived there.'

'The suit he had on looked as if it had been made on the Continent, probably Switzerland or Italy.'

'You noticed that? The maker's label was inside the jacket — Arturo Lagani, Via Umberto, Milan. We're having that checked, too — but I doubt if it'll help. Made to the order of Mr. J. B. Smith. There's probably thousands of J. B. Smiths.'

I sat there thinking. 'The man with the cadaverous face and the small scar on his chin . . . '

'Yes?'

'I'm wondering if he fits in somewhere. I told you he went into a phone booth and more or less on impulse I yanked the door open in time to hear him saying something about I must be one of them.'

'One of who — or is it whom? Doesn't matter. I suppose you haven't any idea what he meant?'

'None. The man who made the call in the hotel wasn't the fellow in the Jag — whom I never saw in my life before he let his cannons off at me.'

'Odd, though, this chap making that call. Pity you weren't able to find out more about that.'

'I wondered if he had got me mixed up with somebody else,' I said. 'Now . . . ' I shrugged.

'Now it has a somewhat different aspect,' Power said. 'This cadaverous chap — was he staying in the hotel?'

'I don't know. The hotel can answer that better.'

Power spoke into a phone. A pause, then he was through. He spoke again, listened and replaced the receiver. 'They say no, he wasn't a guest there. The barman remembers him because he left his drink and didn't come back for it, but he says he never saw him before and doesn't know who he is.'

'We seem to be running into a dead-end street at every turn, inspector.'

'Looks like that — but, never fear, we'll find a way out,' replied Power impassively.

I said slowly: 'So he didn't go back for his drink. I wonder . . . '

'What?'

'If he had anything to do with the driver of the E-type.'

'Set him on you, eh? It's a thought.'

'That's all it is, though.'

'True. Still, we'll see if we can trace him. I take it you're staying on in Thetford for the time being?'

'For a day or two while I contact my client in New York.'

'About this Ben Leffiney, you mean?'

The sergeant, who had come in, said: 'I know old Ben fairly well, though he hasn't been in town much lately. I thought he must be poorly, but from what I've gathered since it seems he was just poor.' The sergeant smiled as if he thought he had made a joke. Maybe he had.

'Well, if he waits a bit he'll not need to worry about that, it seems,' remarked

Power. 'Not that his little affairs are any concern of ours — we've got other fish to fry. If we can catch them, that is.'

I said: 'I suppose you want a signed statement?'

'Better have it, yes. It'll not take you long — forty minutes or so. Sergeant'll see to it.'

Power rose and stretched himself. 'I'll be having a pint in the bar of your hotel, if you care to join me later.'

'I'll do that.' A thought stirred in my mind and I added: 'Fingerprints — anything there?'

Power turned, his eyes twinkling. 'I'd have been a mite disappointed if you'd failed to ask that. We put his dabs on the telephoto, circulated them a bit. New Scotland Yard came on the blower just before we started our little chat.'

'And?'

'Our friend Smith was half-Swedish and half-English and was variously known as Raoul Nielson, Manfred Jorgensen and Frederick Arthur Banks. He is or was an international smuggler of stolen antiques.'

'Well, well,' I said.

'You don't know anything about the antique smuggling racket yourself, Mr. Shand?'

'A little, yes.'

'I thought you might,' said Power. There was an odd inflexion in his voice.

'You said that in a rather special way, inspector.'

'That would be because I had a rather special reason. This book . . . ' He slid open a drawer and took out a book, pushing it across the table so that I could read the title: *A Guide to Marks of Origin of British and Irish Silver Plate from the Mid-16th Century to 1963*.

Power went on evenly: 'Fellows engaged in art stealing and smuggling are known as screwsmen and you could say this book is part of their standard literature — required reading, as it were.'

'I haven't read it,' I said.

'No?' He smiled thinly. 'Then perhaps you can explain how it comes to be in your car with your fingerprints on it . . . '

5

I gave him back his recent smile, even more thinly. I had remembered — late, as usual — something I ought to have remembered earlier, when it would have had the value of that simple honesty which the poet esteems so highly. Now it was going to sound as lame as all getout.

Power was eyeing me almost benevolently. 'Dabs which are obviously yours are on the wheel of your car and elsewhere. They match some on this book, which we found on the floor in the back of your car. I assume you have no objection to our taking your prints and making a precise comparison?'

'None whatever — though I can save you the trouble by saying that my prints will certainly be on the book. The guy in the bar dropped it and I picked it up and gave it back to him. I guess that's what you would call a likely story, isn't it?'

'Perhaps. Perhaps not. On the other

hand, this book *was* in your car.'

'What made you look?'

He built a steeple with his strong fingers. 'We make a habit of looking into everything. Routine attention to detail. Noseying, some people call it. Makes us unpopular at times.'

'When I picked the book up in the hotel bar I didn't read the title,' I said. 'Afterwards, I simply forgot about it.'

'And this man, he was still in the hotel when you left?'

'He was.'

'You drive out on the Brandon road where you are shot at by this chap in the Jag, spend some time first with Ben Leffiney and then with Canon Varley, drive back towards Oak Hall Farm and find this fellow dead in his Jag?'

'I've said all that.'

'And somehow this book finds its way into your car.'

'So it seems.'

'How?'

I shrugged. 'Your guess is as good as mine, inspector.'

'Let's have yours, anyway.'

'I can only conclude that it was put there after I left my own car to walk across to the Jaguar.'

'Sounds thin, wouldn't you say?'

'Damned thin, but I can't think of anything better.' A constable brought in two mugs of tea; the stuff had the general appearance of liquid leather, but Power seemed to like it. I lit a cigarette and said levelly: 'I quite simply forgot about picking up the book until you waved it at me. I guess that's unfortunate — for me.'

'In certain circumstances it might be.'

'What circumstances?'

'Assuming a circumstance in which you shot this chap.'

'You'd have to find the murder weapon, though . . . ' I broke off, then went on: 'It looks altogether too much like an attempt to switch your investigations in the wrong direction, doesn't it?'

'Go on, Mr. Shand.'

'The book belonged to the man with the cadaverous face. It turns up on the floor of my car — after the guy in the E-type has been shot dead. It could have been planted while I left my car to go into the forest clearing. If it was that could make the man in the bar the killer.'

'You're putting up a nice line in defence submission.'

'It figures,' I said doggedly. 'He had all the time in the world to drive out along that road and kill the second fellow — while I was with Ben Leffiney and the rector.'

'And his motive?'

I didn't answer directly. Instead, I said: 'Do you think *I* had one?'

Power rubbed his heavy jaw reflectively. One side of his mouth made a faint twitch. 'No, I don't,' he said. 'And nobody kills anybody without a motive unless he's mentally deranged — and I haven't impugned your sanity.'

'Thanks,' I said drily.

Power went on as if I hadn't spoken. 'I forgot to tell *you* something, Mr. Shand. I had a chat on the phone with Detective Chief Superintendent Logan at the Yard. He seems to think rather well of you — also one of the special security chaps, George Carruthers. Apparently you co-operated with them on a rather interesting case. Before you started up in business over here.'

'Last summer,' I said.

'So they mentioned. They say you're an independent chap, sometimes damned difficult and generally inclined to take a line of your own.' Power grinned. 'They also say you're to be trusted.'

'The unsolicited tribute is much appreciated.'

'Comes at the right moment, eh? One other thing. They appear to entertain a pretty high opinion of your abilities, which is why I'm going along with your theory that the fellow with the cadaverous face is probably the murderer.' Another grin came. 'Not that I ever seriously considered you in the rôle.'

'You kept that well hidden,' I said feelingly.

'Had to put the questions, see how you reacted and so on. Some chaps might have jumped to conclusions because you didn't mention picking up that book. Well, it *did* call for an explanation. Yours fits. People don't always remember every single thing . . . if they do we get really suspicious. Only the guilty think of everything — or try to.'

I stubbed out my cigarette, reached absently for another and decided against it. I smoke too much, anyway. 'What do you think is behind the killing, inspector — a clash between rival art stealing gangs?'

'You're jumping the gun, getting ahead too fast. But, yes, something like that. We'll have to look around, eh?'

'I don't pretend to know the set-up in detail, but I understand that something like £25,000,000 worth of antiques are currently missing in this country alone,' I said.

'Correct. So far as the police are concerned, we have mounting evidence that a high proportion of the stuff has already been smuggled to South America, Europe and, to a much lesser extent, the United States.'

'These gangs,' I said, 'they're not big, are they?'

'No, they don't work that way. Two screwsmen — three or four at the most for a really big job. But the operations are getting too serious for comfort. Loss adjusters estimate that in one year art and antique robberies have risen more than thirty per cent. In Britain — which is still the biggest reservoir of fine art in the world.'

'The gangs have to sell it to somebody,' I said. 'How about that?'

'Well, London is the headquarters of the international art trade — nearly five hundred antique dealers, a hundred and sixty picture dealers, three hundred and fifty art dealers and no end of junk shops in the Metropolitan area alone. Now, of course, there are plenty of honest dealers — but there are also some of the other kind. Some time ago Scotland Yard formed a special team to investigate art steals. They think it more than likely that large sums of 'bent' money — the proceeds of bank raids and wage snatches and suchlike — find their way to a few crooked dealers who then use the money to finance further robberies.' Power made a sardonic smile. 'Nothing better than an antique business for cover.'

'There's a growing American market,' I said. 'Some of the world's richest art collectors live there and I dare say many aren't over-worried about the origin of rare antiques. But I don't think the stuff goes through New York — the F.B.I. circulates descriptions of all stolen property. The way I get the picture, Brazil is the place of entry.'

'For a lot of it, yes. One of the problems we're up against is that fine works of art more than a hundred years old and valued at less than £2,000 can leave Britain without an export licence — so a big haul can be got rid of in separate parcels, as it were.'

'I'd have thought another problem would be that policemen don't, as a general thing, know much about antiques,' I said.

Power nodded. 'To get to grips with this thing you really need to know a lot about silver and jade and so on. That's why the Yard set up this specialist team. Still another worrying factor is that most country house hauls are out of the country before we can act — these lads move bloody quick.'

'It looks as if some of them may have moved into this part of Norfolk, inspector.'

Power fingered his blue tie straight, though it already was. 'I'm handling a murder case . . . ' he began.

'Yes, but everything you've said points to either the killer or his victim being mixed-up with art stealing.'

'I agree, but it's subsidiary to the main line of the investigation. In any event, no country house haul has been reported anywhere in this area.'

'Stick around and it may be,' I said.

'We'll keep that in mind all right — but *if* a steal is being planned why should they make things more difficult for themselves by committing murder?'

'There could be several reasons — gang rivalry, hate, envy, anything.'

'Well, we'll be watching out, never fear. You'd better make that statement. See you later, then.' He moved his bulk easily and went out.

I followed in just under three-quarters of an hour. I didn't go straight into the bar but up to my room. The phone rang as I went in. The voice was one I remembered.

'Hello, Logan,' I said. 'We meet again

. . . on long-distance.'

'I hear you're getting involved in police business down there, Shand. It's getting to be a habit with you, as the song says.'

'I'm not singing it. I came here on an entirely different errand.' I told him briefly what it was.

'Just the same, you've got yourself involved,' Logan replied. 'That's why I'm ringing you.'

'What's the reason?'

'We'd like you to work in with us again. How d'you feel about it?'

'I don't see what possible help I can give.'

'We're sending some chaps down there — antique and art specialists. You could be a useful addition.'

'I still don't get it.'

'You will. Grange Manor — a Tudor country house at a place called Farleigh, three miles from where you are, in the forest area of Thetford Warren. Sir James Arkwright's place. He's putting on an exhibition of family treasures. Our fellows will be there, but they're getting known to the screwsmen. Might be useful to have an unknown on hand — you fit.'

'Is that all you want me to do — just stroll around the aristocratic *menage*?'

'And keep your eyes and ears open.'

'I'd need an invitation.'

A dry sound that could have been a chuckle came down the wire. 'I've already fixed it with Sir James. You'll be a wealthy American collector trying to persuade him to sell to you.'

'I love the idea of being thought wealthy.'

'Well, you're not exactly skint, are you?'

'I'm not exactly rich, either. All right, I'll do it for you. When do I show up?'

'Tomorrow at noon. Informal cocktail party, then the viewing.'

'It sounds too simple.'

'I hope it turns out to be,' said Logan. There seemed to be a small hint of anxiety in his voice. I called attention to it.

'We're being pressurized a bit by the top brass,' Logan said. 'There's a hell of a lot of stuff been nicked in the last year or so — and putting God knows how many thousands of pounds worth of stuff on public view is like tempting Providence.'

'This guy with the spare names,' I said. 'Doesn't that give you a lead — about his associates?'

'Nothing, I'm afraid. His previously known chums are still on the Continent, including a couple now in a Spanish jail. We didn't know he was in the country until Power sent his dabs. Obviously, he must have associates here — but we don't think they're the previous lot.'

'Maybe one of them shot him.'

'Perhaps. We don't know.'

'A rival then. Two mobs clashing over the same expected loot.'

'More like it, yes. Unfortunately, we have no knowledge as to who they could be.'

'You must know the identities of some of the screwsmen, surely?'

'Rick Malleson, Charley Hawksworth, Lee Baldry, Fergus Riordan, Tiny Fanshaw and a girl known as The Charmer.'

'You mean you don't know her name?'

'No. She works alone, by the way.'

'Young, I take it.'

'Twenty-eight to thirty. We don't actually know her and she's never been booked, so she can't be accurately described. But we believe she's pulled off several major jobs.'

'A girl . . . ' I said the word slowly. 'How does she operate — I mean what does she use as a front?'

'She sometimes poses as a magazine writer looking for material,' said Logan.

★   ★   ★

I put the phone back and went down to the bar. Power had been in and gone while I was upstairs. Well, I didn't want to speak to him, not just now.

The bar had filled up for the last half-hour rush. Linda Travers wasn't there, though. I drank part of a small Scotch without enthusiasm, almost without being aware of it.

'Hear you've had a somewhat interesting evening, sir.' It was Joe, the whiskered bartender.

'As a matter of fact, I have — how did you know?'

'News travels fast, especially in a small place, sir.'

'I suppose it does. You don't happen to know where Miss Travers is, by any chance?'

'The young lady you were chatting to before you went out? No, she hasn't been in here since dinner.'

I stood there savouring whisky and funny-peculiar thoughts. Then I went out to the reception and asked them to call her room number.

The blonde girl behind the desk said: 'Miss Travers went out about half an hour ago, sir.'

'I suppose you don't know where?'

'Why, yes. She asked how to get to Farleigh village, Mr. Shand.'

'Thanks,' I said thickly.

It was almost ten o'clock when I got there. The village clustered round a wide main street which merely interrupted the road slashing through the towering forest belt. I parked alongside one of the three inns as a couple of loose-limbed fellows came out of the front entrance and asked them the way to Grange Manor.

The taller of the two took a cherry-wood pipe from between his remaining half-dozen teeth and told me in an accent I had small trouble translating, but I finally made it.

I was going back to my car when he added: 'You're the second stranger asking the way, sir.'

'Oh?'

'That's right. Twice we been asked. The first as we went into the pub and you as we came out.'

'Who asked first — a girl?'

'No, wasn't no young lady. A man — a furinner he was. French or German or summat like that.'

'How long since?'

'Not long, not more'n half an hour. Must be having a lot of strange folk up at the Manor.'

I drove on, fast. Beyond the village a lane joined the 'B' road and Grange Manor was supposed to be about a half-mile down it. In fact, it seemed longer. A countryman's mile?

A drive swept in a massive arc through rolling parkland, finishing on a wide gravelled square in front of the house. No lights showed. I found the doorbell and touched it. I could hear the ringing inside the dark house. Nothing else. I put my thumb hard on the push and kept it there for what seemed like a minute. Nothing happened again. A thin drizzle began to fall. Then a wind sprang up, soughing through the trees and driving the rain against the backs of my legs. I went along the front of the house — and stopped suddenly. I was on the outside of a wide window with leaded panes and one of the panes was open and moving slightly in the wind because it was off its slotted rod.

Inside it was virtually pitch dark and I hadn't brought a flash with me, but no sound came from the room. I got the window fully open and thrust a leg over the sill. Nobody came at me triggering a gun or waving a medieval battleaxe.

I put both feet on the floor and started walking with my hands fanned out so that I wouldn't trip over the unseen furniture. What I actually tripped over was something bulky and soft lying on the floor. I pitched headlong to the carpet, rolling over and going for the gun I wasn't wearing. I could hear myself breathing in a harsh rustle of air. Still nothing happened.

There must be a wall behind me. I moved backwards, one hand probing, until I touched it. I found the switch and snapped it down. Light jumped from a huge electrolier. A long refectory table stood in the middle of the floor and down one side of the room a series of lesser tables were ranged. Cards with typed notes were on the tables — nothing else.

Sprawled on the floor with one leg buckled under him was the pyjama-clad body of a man who could be on the brink of the sixtieth birthday he was never going to see because there was a knife buried deeply between his shoulder-blades.

6

I went down on one knee and moved him slightly, enough to see his face. A lean, finely-chiselled faced with a small grey moustache, neatly trimmed. On the third finger of his left hand was a gold signet ring with the centre oblong inscribed *JA*. I was looking at the late Sir James Arkwright.

My breathing sounded like the risen wind in my ears. I went out of the room into an immense reception hall with dark oak panelling and knightly armour which had long ceased to shine. The silence was uncanny and inexplicable. There had to be somebody around the place, only there wasn't.

A stairway curved upwards and vanished in the gloom. I found more lights and got them on, staring round the hall. Doors led off. I opened three on silent rooms. The fourth showed me a passage; no carpet now, only polished linoleum. I walked down it and pushed at the first door I came to and stopped in my tracks.

There were five persons in the room, gagged and corded to as many straight-backed chairs: a stout party with a face ruddier than a sunset who looked as if he could be the butler, a dumpy woman who could be the housekeeper or the cook, a youngish fellow wearing chauffeur uniform and a couple of maids.

I cut them free and all five tried to speak at once. The result was a chorus of croaks. The butler recovered the power of movement first. He tottered to the sideboard and poured himself a schooner of what looked like Napoleon brandy straight from cobwebbed cellars below the castle moat. The life-giving fluid brought coherency to his speech as well as an added flush to his florid features.

'Who . . . who are you, sir?'

'A private investigator with an invitation to visit here tomorrow, only I came tonight instead.'

He splayed a veined hand on the table. 'Thank God you *did* come, sir . . . I fear the young maids were ready to pass out . . . '

One of them, a girl with a pointed chin and wide blue eyes, ran to me and put her head against my chest, sobbing.

'Come, come Janet,' said the Old Retainer. 'Pull yourself together, my girl.'

The chauffeur put a cigarette between small white teeth, nibbled on it and said: 'How do we know you're who you say you are?'

'If I was what you seem to be thinking I am, you'd still be trussed to that chair,' I said evenly.

'That's all very well, but . . . '

The butler turned imperiously, like a stout Caesar quelling an unseemly heckler in the Roman Forum. 'Can't you see that this gentleman is a gentleman, Charles?' he said coldly. I reflected wryly that he was the first man who had ever called me that.

I said: 'I'd like a word with you — in private.'

The chauffeur sneered. 'And you,' I added.

The housekeeper said: 'I'll take the

maids to the kitchen, sir, and make a nice hot cup of tea.'

When they had gone I said without preamble: 'Sir James is dead. Somebody put a knife straight into his back. He's on the library floor . . . '

The butler swayed, his eyes bulging. 'Sir James dead . . . *murdered* . . . '

'I'm afraid so, Mr . . . ?'

'Meedes, sir. Septimus Meedes.' He spelt the name out.

The chauffeur, who was inhaling cigarette smoke, coughed loosely on it.

Before he could speak, I said: 'Do you mind telling me what happened before I got here, Mr. Meedes?'

The butler answered shakingly: 'There was a ring at the doorbell. I answered it in person. A man wearing a mask, a sort of stocking pulled down over his face, pushed a pistol into my chest and told me to keep quiet. He forced me back down the hall and into my pantry, where we are now, sir. Then he compelled me to summon the rest of the staff and menaced them with the revolver.'

I didn't know whether Septimus

Meedes knew the difference between a revolver and an automatic, but just now it didn't matter. I said: 'Then what?'

'He compelled Charles to tie-up the housekeeper, the maids and myself. Then he himself bound Charles to a chair and went out.'

'I see. Where was the rest of the household while all this was going on?'

'There was only Sir James, sir, and he had retired early. Lady Arkwright is in London and is expected back in the morning with some of the party for the art exhibition.'

'Was there any other intruder — apart from this guy with the stocking mask?'

The butler stared. 'I didn't see anyone, sir.'

'Did you hear anything, like a car?'

'Yes — it's rather odd, now I come to think of it. Before I answered the door I heard a car drive up. Sometime later I fancied I heard another. But that's not all. There was another sound . . . '

'What kind of sound?'

'It was while we were being tied-up. It

71

. . . well, it sounded like some kind of small aircraft.'

'*I* heard it,' the chauffeur said. 'It stopped, but some time after this masked fellow left it started up again, quite near it was. We all heard it. Then it faded and a few minutes later I heard a car. Sounded like a big job, a three or four litre I'd say.' He stared at me from very bright eyes. 'If Sir James was in bed how did he come to be in the library?' He asked the question in a nasty tone.

'He probably heard the sounds, too, and came down to see what was going on, I imagine. Then . . . ' I let the rest of it go.

'You didn't tell us your name,' said the chauffeur with a notable lack of friendliness.

'Dale Shand.' I turned to the faithful retainer. 'I'd like to call the police on your phone, if I may.'

'Of course, sir.' He nodded at a shelf near the window.

I was crossing the room when I heard the sound — a high drone like a plane engine revving before take-off. I slammed the side window wide open and got through it, dropping on to a path which ran down one side of the house, extending to the lawn.

If there was a bigger lawn I had never seen it. The plane was going down it lengthwise. When I reached the rim of the closely-mown grass it was already airborne. The drizzle and the wind had gone and in the next instant the darkness lightened as a full moon moved free of cloud.

For an instant it lit up the fuselage. It was a small plane, a Piper Cherokee. I could even read the lettering — O OMOC. Then it was fully up and going through the cloudbank.

I went back into the house, running. I had never run faster, not even at college in the hundred yards sprint. The butler's eyes were like twin gooseberries. His mouth opened and closed and opened again, gaping on its hinges. I yanked the telephone up and dialled 999.

A cool voice said: 'Which service do you require, sir?'

'Police.'

'You're through, sir.'

Another voice. I didn't know it. 'Constable Dodsley, Farleigh police station . . . '

'Damn,' I said. I got back to the operator. 'Sorry — I want the police at Thetford.'

'You should've said, sir. Hold on and I'll get them for you.'

Seconds tramped by, like prisoners shackled to ball and chain. The sergeant came on the line.

I said: 'Shand here. Is Detective Inspector Power around?'

'Yes, Mr. Shand. I'll put him on.'

Power's voice, heavy but not wholly imperturbable. 'What's happened?'

I told him the lot, sub-edited down to about five short paragraphs, and finished: 'A Piper Cherokee plane took off from the lawn of the Arkwright place. A small plane with markings. I read them. The index is O OMOC . . . '

'The double O prefix means it's a Belgian plane,' said Power. 'I'll have a squad car out there in quick-sticks. Don't tell me anything else just now — I'll see if we can stop that bloody plane getting out of the country.'

'If that's what he's doing he'll be over the North Sea coast in minutes from now,' I replied.

'No doubt, but we have to try. There are methods.' He clicked the receiver down.

I looked round the butler's pantry. The housekeeper and the maids were back. They had to be told now, in case one of them went into the library and threw a fit of the vapours, if serving maids still had the vapours. They took it better than I had expected.

The young chauffeur came through the doorway. 'I've been in . . . ' he began.

'I hope you haven't touched anything,' I growled.

'I know better than that,' he said.

The butler eyed me with anxious, if pop-eyed solemnity. 'You have the look of a gentleman who could use a drink, sir, if you will pardon the observation . . . '

'You've got yourself a free pardon,' I said. 'But I don't think I will, though.'

The squad car arrived and I watched them go to work. I made a preliminary statement and drifted back into the butler's pantry. The telephone rang. In the silence which had descended upon us it sounded like the crack of doom.

Power was on the wire. His voice told me the worst. 'The plane's beyond limits. We can't get it back.'

'Hell! The fellow in it cleaned out the entire art collection as well as being mixed-up in the murder of Arkwright.'

'What d'you mean — mixed up in it?'

'I told you a masked guy got in here. The butler and the chauffeur heard a car. It's my guess he went away in it after loading the plane. And that's not all.'

'You didn't indicate there was something else, Shand.' His voice had a crackle like trodden egg-shells.

'You didn't give me much time when I was on before. There was a second car here, but it isn't out front. It's probably stashed away somewhere out of sight.' I hesitated, then said: 'I'm guessing that the girl who arrived in it is on that plane . . . '

'Damn it all — what girl?' roared Power.

'Unless I've got it all wrong, a girl

named Linda Travers.'

'For God's sake, who *is* she?'

'A girl staying in the hotel I'm at. We met briefly. She said she was a magazine writer.'

Power said something in basic Anglo-Saxon. Rather less than fifteen minutes later he was out at the Manor.

'A three-handed job,' he said. 'The screwsman moves in with a gun and the girl follows, going straight into the room where the collection is on display. The pilot has the plane waiting on the bloody great lawn.'

'You think Linda Travers is the girl you call The Charmer?'

'Who else,' He looked dourly at me. 'Unless you've got some other information you haven't mentioned.'

'No, but I have the feeling *you* may be jumping the gun this time.'

'Look — we know there's a woman in the art-stealing business and we know she sometimes poses as a magazine writer.'

'It could be coincidence.'

'Everything fits . . . ' He stopped and rubbed his jaw. 'If she *isn't* involved what are you suggesting?'

'I'm not suggesting anything just at this moment. What I think is that we could establish whether Miss Travers is or is not what she claims to be.'

'Yes, we can do that.'

I looked round the room and the police still working in it methodically with their cameras and graphite powder and chalk. 'You don't need me immediately, inspector — suppose I go back to the hotel and take a look at her room?'

'One of the constables will have to accompany you.'

'Sure. If she's a journalist she'll have something among her possessions.'

'All right.' He called one of the officers over.

I drove back into Thetford and we went up to her room. On a table in the window bay was a portable Underwood 18 with a sheet of quarto paper still in the platen. It read like the start of an article. Behind the portable was a letter addressing her as *Dear Linda* and signed by the Features Editor. The letter heading was that of the National

Magazine Publishing Corporation. Below it was a list of the company's publications and a Fleet Street address. There was also a list of the directors, including the managing director. I found his private address, not without trouble, and got him on the telephone. I had just put the receiver down when the phone rang.

It was Power. 'Well, did you find anything?' he demanded.

'She's an accredited journalist working full-time as a features writer for the National Magazine Publishing Corporation. I've just been through to the managing director. He vouches for her without reservations.'

'That means only one thing, then — she must have arrived in the middle of the robbery and they've kidnapped her.'

'Yes. She could identify them, including the murderer. Not necessarily by names, but she would know them again.'

Power said: 'The plane's been traced. An RAF Shackleton went out. We've just had a radio message that a small plane with the OO prefix crossed the French coast about fifty miles south of Calais. It was also *going* south. We've contacted the French authorities, also Interpol.'

'What's the chances?'

'Can't say, we'll have to wait. I'm coming back to Thetford. You can wait for me at the police station.'

I put the phone down and re-read what she had written. It was only a handful of sentences and seemed like the start of a general introduction. The table had a long shallow drawer. I pulled it out and saw a notebook, two ballpoint pens and some 10½ × 8½ buff-coloured envelopes. The notebook contained only about a dozen pages of writing, in scrawled longhand with shorthand interpolations and it wasn't easy to read. I went back to the beginning and tried again, working slowly through it. I could hear myself making a low whistle. She hadn't come to Norfolk merely to write-up the mansions of the landed gentry — she was working on what was clearly intended to be an exposé of the art-stealing racket. And the recurring name was mine . . .

I remembered the sudden tightness and

the odd tone in her voice when we talked in the hotel bar. It had irritated me at the time, but now I understood. She thought I was down here as one of the gang, probably the Big Shot. Well, she knew better now — for as long as they let her go on living. I felt a cold sag at my stomach. For God's sake, we *couldn't* leave her to it.

The boyish constable who had come with me said: 'You look a bit worried, sir.'

'More than a bit.' I told him what was in the notebook.

'We'd better get back to the station,' he said.

Power was already there, on the telephone. I paced restlessly about the room, waiting.

When he finished his call he said: 'The plane's landed — on a disused airstrip. When the authorities got there the occupants had gone.'

'They'll kill her,' I said harshly.

'Perhaps, but they haven't done it yet. A farm worker saw the plane come in. There was a car waiting, a red-and-white Alfa-Romeo with an Italian registration. They didn't transfer to it, though. They

81

simply talked with the driver and then took off for Milan. The peasant, who was on the other side of a hedge, heard them say it . . . he couldn't make out the rest because he speaks hardly any English.'

I said: 'Somehow, we've got to stop them.'

'We're doing everything possible, Shand.' He eyed me directly. 'You seem to be worried almost in a personal sense.'

'I liked the look of her. I don't care to think . . . '

'Then don't.'

'That's easier said than done.'

'Yes, it is — but that sort of thinking isn't going to help.'

'Do you want me to make another statement?'

'It'll do in the morning.'

'No, I'll make a detailed one now.'

He shrugged. I made the statement, signed it and went back to the hotel. I called Nancy at her apartment in St. John's Wood, checked-out, got into my car and drove to London. When I got to Heathrow she had fixed everything.

Thirty-seven minutes later I was on the night flight to Milan.

7

It was crazy. I was looking for the owner of one particular Alfa-Romeo in a city which probably had them by the gross.

But not totally crazy. I had a friend who lived in a terra-cotta apartment block within sight of the great cathedral they started building five hundred years ago and still haven't finished. Alberto Fressini, a dark-haired and smiling Milanese who used to be a police lieutenant and was now in the same lunatic business as myself. That was why I was in Milan. Nancy had phoned him while I was driving to London and now he was waiting for me.

A taxi dropped me off on the Via Santa Maria Maggiore and he had the door open before I could ring the bell.

'Dale! So you have arrive, eh?' He relapsed into Italian. '*Questo mi piace assai*!'

'I'll like it even better if you can give

me a lead,' I said.

'You tell Alberto what you want and we see what can be done.' His dazzling smile flashed. 'Meanwhile, it is after four o'clock in the morning and you are beyond the doubt a little tired and maybe you like a drink.'

He spread both his arms briefly. 'I am — how you say? — on the wagon, so I drink only the coffee. But I keep the *vino* and the whisky for my guests.'

'Coffee,' I said.

While he made it I told him what had happened — all of it. His boyish face became animated; it was the kind of case that would fascinate him.

This Signor Leffiney — I find him interesting.'

'Very — but it's the art steal and, more particularly, the girl I'm troubled about.'

He grinned. 'Money, *amico* — always poor Alberto is interested in the money, but never do I meet one who will inherit untold millions. The good farmer is what you call the lucky stiff, eh?'

'When old man Leffiney dies, yeah. It might be years ahead.' I drank some of the coffee and went on: 'What do you know about the art-stealing racket?'

'In Milano very little. You have come to the wrong country. Switzerland is better.'

'I thought you were going to say Brazil or some such place. Why Switzerland?'

'Just at this time there is an international smuggling ring operating from a villa near Lugano. Very undercover, but it is there. The police they know this, but never are they able to get the proof.'

I shifted my weight irritably. 'These people were heading for Milan — unless the farm worker misheard.'

'And Milano she is not far from the Swiss frontier,' Alberto said gently.

'Why should they make for Milan at all? They'd have to pass over Lugano, or close enough, to get here. And there's a landing strip near the lake, isn't there?'

'My good friend, there could be any one of a number of most excellent reasons, could there not? Some business in Milano — perhaps an important contact to pick up.'

'An international dealer waiting here to be taken to Lugano, you mean? A fellow ready to buy the stuff?'

'It is a possibility. Describe the man you found shot in the forest.'

I told him, as closely as I could remember. He shook his head. 'I do not know such a one, Dale. Now the other — in the detail.'

'A tall guy, cadaverous face . . . '

'Cadav . . . what is this you say?'

'A long kind of face with a small puckered scar on the chin . . . ' I stopped.

Alberto gestured widely. 'So well you do to come to me, *amico*. Unless it is the coincidence, I know this man. He was here in Milano no more than a week ago, staying at the Albergo Magnani, which is most expensive. Helmut Borge. He is one of this smuggling ring.'

'What kind of smuggling?'

'Many kinds. Contraband cigarettes in bulk, currency, gold — and, more recently, the smuggling into South America of art works and antiques, particularly from England.'

'How do you come by this knowledge?' I asked curiously.

'I still have the friends in the police.

They know all this, though they are not yet in a position to prove anything, as I have explained.'

'But if they have strong grounds for suspicion?'

'Suspicion it is not enough, especially as this villa is occupied by one of wealth and influence, what the English call the VIP.'

'Who?'

'A Spaniard. His name is Juan Francesco. A financier — which is a rôle most convenient. He has offices in Zurich. It is not simple for the police to enter his villa without proof.'

'What's he like in a personal sense?'

'I have never seen him — not even his picture, which does not appear in the newspapers. He is careful to avoid all publicity. A photographer who tried to take his picture finished without the picture and also without his camera.'

'You mean this guy Francesco smashed it?'

'Not Francesco, no. One of his secretaries — wherever he goes there are always two secretaries.' Another grin moved on Alberto's handsome face. 'I hear they are most formidable secretaries.'

'Bodyguards or strong-arm men, you mean?'

'*Si* — so I think.'

'How old is this Francesco?'

'Not old, perhaps forty-five. There are those who call him El Rapier because he is the great expert in the art of fencing.'

'And Borge is involved with him?'

'I do not know — but thees man he has been here and the villa is not far. It seem like what you call the connection.' He poured more coffee, watching me expectantly.

'How'd you like to drive me to Lugano?' I said.

Alberto laughed. 'That is what I hope you say. You mean within the next ten minutes?'

'Fine.'

'Your *passaporto* — it is in the good order?'

'Fine.'

'Then we go,' cried Alberto jubilantly. He slid open the door of a rosewood desk, took out two .32 automatic pistols with ribbed rubber grips and handed one to me. 'Now that you have become *l'investigatore privato* in England you will, of necessity, be unarmed — so I make the correction!'

I said nothing until we were three miles out of Milan going north for the Swiss frontier. We were in an all-white Fiat Samantha styled by Vignale, and Alberto drove it with the special flair Italians seem to have for cars, though without the conscious recklessness you can see too much of in this country. The road was empty at this hour and the rushing air had the peculiar aromatic warmth which is the first thing you notice when you come to Italy.

He eased his foot off the pedal to take a long righthand bend. Above the whine of the transmission I said: 'When we get there you'd better keep somewhat in the background, Alberto.'

Cutting the speed down to the low fifties he said: '*Che cosa vuol dire?*'

'It means what I said — you keep out of this business.'

Without turning his handsome head, he said: 'So I am to be nothing more than the chauffeur, eh?'

'That's right.'

'You permit me to drive you to this villa and then deny me the action?'

'Right again.'

'Like the *signorina* who give you the big eye but withhold the ultimate pleasure?'

'In this case the operative word is more likely to be danger.'

'*Bella*!' said Alberto.

'Look, I can't invite you to involve yourself in dangerous business on my behalf.'

His long fingers drummed lightly on the steering wheel. 'I invite myself,' he announced.

'These men have already killed. They'll stop at nothing.'

'And you think I will let you go in alone — is that what you think, my good friend?'

'No, I don't think that. Also, I value your willingness to come in with me. But it's too much to ask.'

'You do not have to ask it, Dale,' he answered quietly. 'You are my friend and one owes something to one's friends.'

'Maybe, but . . . '

'We now approach the frontier,' said Alberto, as if I hadn't spoken.

Five minutes later we were in Switzerland, though at first the transition means little because neither the climate nor the language change in the southern half of this incredibly lovely country. The first grey streaks of dawn thrust questing fingers across the sky, high above the snow-tipped peak of distant St. Moritz. Down below the lake was stilled, lying like an unsheathed sword, a dull silver which would soon be aquamarine blue — but not just yet.

We came to Lugano and swept east on the Paradiso promenade which follows the great curve of the lakeshore, on past the Lido which, in a few hours, would be jammed with magnificent sun-bronzed youth and the middle-aged men cutting less magnificent figures in swim briefs. Up beyond the Hotel Villa Castagnola the promenade ends abruptly in a flurry of small shops and a suddenly narrowed roadway which plunges almost to the wooded shoreline. We went down it, driving more slowly now, with the lights cut out.

Alberto said: 'The Villa Manfredi is where we go. It is no more than a few kilos from here.'

'You've seen it before?'

'*Si*, once only. I come here for a weekend with a most beautiful *signorina* . . . .' He blew a kiss off the tips of his fingers. 'We take an excursion on the lake and the villa is pointed out to us as being most interesting.' He grinned. 'The guide is, of course, unaware just how interesting it really is.'

The road dipped sharply. Alberto cut the engine out now and we drifted down with no more sound than the slapping of tyres. Then that ceased as we stopped and went forward on foot. The villa stood on a green slope rising from the edge of the lake. There was a small jetty hacked out of the rock. A red and white Alfa Romeo stood on the rolled gravel apron. We had come to the right place.

Lights showed thinly from behind several shuttered windows. Alberto whispered: 'You are in charge, *amico* — what do we do?'

I stood looking at the villa. A frontal approach with the .32 automatics? Too chancy. We had no way of knowing how many men were in the place. If we were outnumbered some of them could take us from the rear. There had to be another way in. I looked back along the narrow roadway. There was a gate in the shade of tall trees. I touched Alberto's arm.

'You have found a way?' he asked.

'I'm not sure, we'll see.' I walked along the road to the gap in the trees. There was a path beyond the gate, winding and dipping to the water's edge. We went down it, testing every step. A dislodged stone might make enough noise to be heard in the total silence, especially if it plopped into the lake. We didn't dislodge one.

The path was flanked by trees whose interlaced branches met like a ragged roof, making a deep green tunnel. There was a curve to the left. Then, suddenly, we were out in the open with nothing but the vastness of the lake and the little jetty thrusting its arm above the water.

Alberto looked at me, not speaking.

I said: 'If we can get on to the jetty we should be able to find a way into the villa — from below.'

'*Come?*'

'If we wade a few yards out into the lake we can climb up the side of the jetty.'

'*Andiamo avanti*,' grinned Alberto.

'How deep is it?'

'If we do not go more than a little way the lake is shallow. After that it is most deep.'

'We won't need to go far,' I said.

In fact, the water was up to my thighs by the time I reached the under-structure of the jetty. Steel pillars drove down into the bed of the lake. I went up one of them, clambered on to the wood platform and waited until Alberto hauled himself up alongside me. There was no sound anywhere except the faint impact of barely moving lakewater. The pier and a narrow tunnel of water vanished below the villa, through a crescent-shaped archway. It ended in an oval basin on which a motor cruiser was moored. At the rear of the basin was a concrete platform and a door.

I turned the trigger-handle inch by inch and leaned a shoulder on the panels. The door opened inwards on impenetrable blackness. I took the gun out, freed the safety-catch and held it in my right hand while I used the other to thumb the switch of a pencil-flash. A thin white beam probed ahead. It showed us stone steps spiralling upwards to another door. I could hear my heartbeats; they were like small thunder, but nobody else would be able to hear them.

I snapped off the light and we started up the steps, single-file. There were thirty-one steps, but they seemed like a hundred. If men came through the door at the top we were finished, and I knew it. Maybe we could shoot somebody first — but we'd never get away.

We were on the penultimate step when I heard the sound and froze in my tracks. It was a footfall beyond the door. Then a voice, muffled but audible.

'There's nothing we want from the cruiser, I brought everything up.' It sounded like the voice of the man with the cadaverous face, Helmut Borge.

The footsteps went away. I waited for a small eternity. Nothing. I went up the last step. I didn't risk another flash. I used one hand to explore the surface of the door until I found the handle. It turned and the door moved. I inched it open, enough to walk through.

We were in a corridor. There was no electric light on, but it wasn't needed because now the pale half-light of dawn was spearing through the single high window.

The floor was dusty and several packing crates were stacked along one of the walls. I guessed that the corridor's sole use was as an access to the steps leading down to the mooring basin. At the other end the corridor opened on to a landing, but I didn't go to it immediately. There was a side door midway down the passage and from behind it came a small, inarticulate sound, a voice-sound. I stopped and tried the handle. The door was locked. I took a slim oblong of celluloid from behind the money in my billfold and used it on the mechanism. The trick usually works fairly easily. But this time I thought it wasn't; then there was the small click of the wards going back. I palmed my free hand on the panels and the door opened.

The shuttered room was like a wall of blackness. I slid round the door, waited for Alberto, then closed it and snapped the flash on, fanning the room in an arc of light. It was empty except for an iron bedstead with brass knobs on the posts.

Linda Travers was lying on it. She seemed to be unconscious.

8

She wasn't, though. I went across the room and pointed the torch straight down. Her eyes were open but they weren't focusing right. An incoherent mumbling came from her.

'She is ill,' whispered Alberto.

I crossed to the window and got one of the heavy shutters open without making noise, letting in some of the dawn, enough to see by. When I got back to the bed she was stirring uneasily. Her rumpled mini skirt was showing her legs, but I wasn't looking at them; I was looking at her right arm, outflung so that the clenched hand dangled over the side of the bed. There were small punctures in it.

'She's been drugged,' I said. 'But she's coming round. Help me get her off the bed.'

'If she falls they will hear, *amico*.'

'We'd better make sure she doesn't, then,' I said.

We stood her on her feet. I pulled the mattress off the bed and spread it on the floor while Alberto held on to her. Then we walked her up and down on it, a few jerky steps at a time. After a while her eyes began to focus and her mouth opened. I clapped a hand over it.

'Don't yell, don't even speak — not yet.'

We walked her up and down again. The heavy dragging of her feet lightened. Suddenly, she clung to me, both arms round my neck. She started sobbing. I put my big hand across her mouth again and said: 'If you want to cry do it quietly.'

She nodded. The pupils of her eyes were coming back to normal. I took my hand away and said: 'Can you talk now?'

'Yes . . . '

'Do it in a whisper.'

We sat on the edge of the bed, one on either side of her. I said: 'This is a very good friend, Alberto Fressini.'

'How . . . how did you find me?' she asked.

'We'll tell you later. How many men are there in this place?'

'I . . . I'm not sure. A man named Borge comes in here with a . . . a syringe, a hypodermic. I haven't seen any others, but I've heard voices.'

'Have they done anything else to you, Linda?'

'No,' she said in a low voice. 'I haven't been completely unconscious . . . I'd have known.'

'What were they going to do — finally?'

She trembled violently. 'I think they mean to kill me. But the one who comes in here said nothing could be done until someone else arrives or phones an order . . . '

'A man called Francesco?'

'He didn't use that name.'

'A man they call El Rapier?'

'Yes . . . that was the name. You *know* him?'

'Not yet.' I thought for a second, then said: 'It must be nearly time for Borge to come back with his hypodermic.'

Another tremor ran through her. 'Don't let him . . . '

'We won't,' I said. 'Can you walk now?'

'I think so.' She stood up, unsteadily,

but she was going to be all right.

'Watch her,' I said.

I went out into the corridor. There was another door on the opposite side. It opened on to a flight of emergency stairs. I went back and said: 'I've found a way out. Take her back to the car, Alberto.'

'And you, my good friend?' Alberto asked quietly.

'I'll follow.'

'What are you going to do?'

'Find out something.'

'What?'

'Whatever there is to find. I'm going into the occupied part of the villa to listen. I'll take care they don't see me.'

'It is dangerous, *amico*. There should be two of us. Better than one, eh?'

'Much better, but somebody has to get Miss Travers out of here. That's your job.'

'If you do not join us in five minutes I come back.'

'Give me ten.'

'As you wish.' Alberto turned to Linda Travers. '*Posso accompagnarla a casa, signorina?*'

She stared.

I grinned. 'He's asking if he may see you home?'

'I wish I was going home . . . anywhere but this dreadful place.'

'You will be.'

I walked with them to the head of the emergency stairs, watched them going slowly down. I closed the door and moved on to the landing. It half-circled the central hallway of the villa, almost level with a hanging cluster of lights. The stairway rose up in a graceful sweep, uncarpeted but with soft mats clipped to each step. I started walking down them with the gun held against my thigh. I reached the bottom without sound.

Voices came from behind a brass-studded door. Two voices, but I knew only one, the voice of the cadaverous man I had seen briefly in the bar of a quiet English inn; it seemed like a million years ago, in another age.

The door wasn't on the latch. I could see into the room. Borge was directly in the limited zone of vision; not the other man, whoever he was.

But it was his voice that was speaking

now. 'How much longer do we have to wait for the call?'

'Until it comes, Jiri. Do not be impatient.'

'He ought to be here. Why is he not here, tell me that.'

'El Rapier has his reasons.'

Jiri laughed harshly. 'El Rapier — me, I do not like this funny name.'

'You have not been asked what it is you like or do not like, my friend. You are paid merely to obey orders — and the pay is not small.'

'I am not complaining of the pay . . . '

'It is better you do not complain of anything — especially in *his* hearing,' said Borge suavely. 'He has a way with those who complain.'

There was a scraping sound, then cigarette smoke eddied into view. The man called Jiri said uneasily: 'I repeat I am not making the complaint. I obey the orders without question. Never has he had reason to doubt that. It is just that . . . '

'It is just that you do not like the waiting,' interrupted Borge. 'I do not like it myself, especially as the police are getting a little inquisitive about us, but we have no choice. Besides, he will telephone us. He has said this.'

Borge pushed his cuff back and looked at his watch. 'It is time to give the *fräulein* her medicine again . . . '

'I'd like to give her something else,' said Jiri.

'*Ja*, you like her,' grinned Borge. 'Not that this is unusual. You like anything in the skirts, is it not so?'

'I'd like . . . '

'You would like to add rape to your already not inconsiderable catalogue of crimes,' said Borge. 'That is, of course, unless you have already committed it in the past, which seems more than probable.'

Jiri said in a brittle voice: 'I do not care for this talk, but . . . '

Borge made a laugh. 'Perhaps Juan will give her to you as a plaything . . . but perhaps not.'

'She knows too much. He'll just have her killed.'

'Assuredly — but the point is that

nothing is to be done to her until he gives the directive. Apart, of course, from keeping her under heavy sedation.' While he spoke Borge was charging a long hypodermic. Jiri moved into view alongside him — a younger fellow with stiff, closely-cropped hair above a face whose flattened contours had a Mongol look.

The phone rang. Borge moved right out of vision to answer it. I poked the door open marginally wider. He was speaking. '*Ja* — I understand. Everything is in order. The art treasures have been moved from here, as you ordered . . . ' A pause, then: 'The Swiss authorities have not yet come here. If they do they will find nothing . . . not even the girl.' Another silence, then: 'It shall be done as you wish.'

I heard the small click of the receiver going down on the rest bar. Borge said calmly: 'The troublesome *fräulein* is to be disposed of — immediately. A massive injection this time, then we drop her in the lake. It will be supposed that she was a drug addict . . . so delightfully simple, eh?'

'Where do we join the boss?'

'At . . . ' Borge stopped. His eyes were directly on the door. I had moved it no more than another inch, but he had seen.

I slammed the door wide open and went in. Jiri's hand swept inside his jacket, but I had already fired. The bullet ripped his sleeve open, searing his arm. He yelped, staggering sideways.

'All right, Borge, don't try anything,' I said.

He just stood there with the hypodermic syringe still in his hand. He was smiling and I didn't like it because he had nothing to smile about.

'You have come a long way from Thetford, my friend,' he murmured. 'You must tell us how you know about this place, *ja*?'

I walked a little way into the room. 'Drop that thing you're holding and get both hands above your head.'

He did it. I took Jiri's gun away from him. There was blood on his arm, but the bullet wasn't embedded in it.

I said: 'Who was the character in the armoured E-type?'

Borge shrugged. 'An associate, a somewhat eccentric fellow but useful — up to a point. Regrettably, he went beyond that point.'

'And you killed him?'

'But, of course. It was necessary and we do not shrink from performing necessary tasks.'

'Who *was* he?'

'Do not be impatient, my friend. He was known to us as Raoul Nielsen, though he had other names. A brilliant engineer. He converted the E-type because it delighted his inventive genius. A plaything, you understand? But he was instructed not to use it. Unfortunately, he chose to ignore the instruction. Unfortunate for him, I mean.'

'So you killed him and tried to frame me for it.'

'The idea amused me, Mr. Shand.' He was still smiling. There was something wrong, but I had no notion of what it could be. He moved backwards, still with his hands raised. He was almost flattened against the wall. His right foot lifted fractionally, then came down and he shouted something in German; it sounded like a command. A panel slid open in the wall and a huge Alsatian dog lunged out, soaring at me.

I fired point-blank into its mouth. For a split second the animal seemed to be suspended in mid-air, then it thudded to the parquetry floor and banged into my legs. I was off balance for no more than another split second, but in that time they were on me.

Borge's fist hit me on the temple. I sagged to my knees as he brought his hand down in a chop on my left shoulder. I still had the gun, but now Jiri had a knife at my throat. His flat face was like a twisted mask.

'I kill him, eh?'

Borge grinned. 'Not just yet.' His hand whipped my face, criss-cross. 'The girl — where is she?'

I said nothing.

'Stay with him while I look, Jiri,' Borge said. He was back in minutes, his face tight. 'She has gone. Juan will not be pleased.'

'Let me give him the knife,' said Jiri.

'First the eyes . . . '

Borge stood still, listening. A car sounded somewhere out on the road. It wasn't Alberto's. Just a car going somewhere. But Borge's face was uneasy. 'We get out of here — now,' he said curtly. 'In the cruiser, across the lake to Como.'

Jiri yanked me back on my feet. 'Move, American pig,' he said.

We went the way I had come, up the stairs and along the corridor and down the steps to the jetty. 'Lock him in the cabin,' snapped Borge.

He put a hand under my chin, forcing it up. 'You are American, so I think of a way to dispose of you,' he said. 'Heavy weights attached to your feet and we drop you in the lake and you die like a gangster in one of your Hollywood movies . . . most apt . . . '

9

I went down below with Jiri behind me. He put a foot in the small of my back and kicked me inside and the door closed.

The impact sent me straight across the cabin. I hit the bunk, cannoned off and sprawled on the floor. I had no gun, no way of getting out. I had nothing except time and not much of that. Maybe only minutes while they took the cruiser out into the middle of the lake. I heard the motor cough into life. After a moment the sound settled into a quiet purr. Then we were heading out into the lake. I could see the deep water, blue now under the early morning sun, through the porthole.

I groped mechanically for cigarettes. Much good they were going to do me. Borge and Jiri would be coming down for me, perhaps in seconds now. My hand touched a box of matches. I looked round the cabin. A stack of mixed European newspapers was on a shelf. I pulled one off, set fire to it and rammed it against the wall alongside the door. Flames licked upwards. I tore pages out of more papers and fed them into the blaze.

Footsteps came. Then the sound of the key turning in the lock, and the door opened. Jiri came through, stopped and started a yell. It died in his throat as I kicked a huge mass of blazing paper up into his face.

He reeled back, lost balance and lurched forward, clawing at his face. I hit him just the once, with everything I had. I could feel my fist sink into his belly. A high thin sound like wheezing air gushed from him. He pitched straight down on the floor. The gun he had come in with clattered from him. He went after it, sprawling. I stamped on his outstretched hand. There was a small brittle sound and he screamed.

I went from the cabin, locked the door and raced up the short companion-way. Borge was at the wheel. He heard me in time to jump sideways and dive for my legs as I fired. We went down, locked together and fighting silently but not cleanly. It wasn't the time for the Marquess of Queensberry's rules. The cruiser was uncontrolled, drifting. Borge got both hands under my jaw, driving at the windpipe. I jerked a knee upwards to his groin, rolled clear and started to come back on my feet as a shot sounded below, then a juddering crash.

From the floor Borge yelled: 'Take him, Jiri . . . kill him!'

I kicked Borge in the chest, jumped away as Jiri came up. His broken hand was dangling down his side. He had to shoot left-handed, but I had already jumped at an angle and was going fast down the deck. Spare cans of gasolene were stacked beyond the rise of the cabin roof. I got down behind them, aiming.

Borge shouted: 'He's still on board. We'll just steer for the Italian shore and ram his end of the cruiser into the beach.'

It was a good enough idea. If they rammed the beach hard enough the chances were that I'd be thrown and they could pick me off with ease.

The cruiser was back on course,

gathering speed. I could hear the white-crested water surging past. I crawled on my stomach across the small deck, not sideways but directly to the rails. They didn't come after me. Why should they? They were going to deal with me in their time, not mine.

There was just room between the rails to slide my body through and dive into the lake — and it had better be away from the propellor. I turned, looking back. Nothing except the stacked cans of gasolene. I lay flat, steadied my gun in the crook of an arm and fired five bullets straight into the cans.

They literally blew apart. There was a tremendous blast and a wall of flame tore skywards as I dived. For minutes I didn't look back. I was swimming, the fastest crawl I had ever managed. I could hear a whole series of detonations behind me. When I finally turned the cruiser was a roaring inferno. Two dark figures were silhouetted momentarily against the flames. Then they were leaping outwards in unison.

The Swiss shore neared. I could make out the long sweep of the Paradiso. I came ashore at the private lido of the Villa Castagnola. Far down the front to my left men were shouting. A launch put out. I ran past the hotel, on and on to where we had left the car.

Borge and Jiri were still swimming for the Italian side of the lake. I hoped they weren't going to make it.

★　★　★

We drove back to Milan with Linda Travers crouched under a rug while we crossed into Italy because she didn't have a passport and there was no time to embark on tedious explanations.

A mile past the frontier Alberto stopped and we got her out. An hour later she was in bed drinking coffee with the two of us sat on either side of her.

'You feel much better now, *signorina*, eh?' asked Alberto.

'Much.' She put the cup down on the bedside table and took our hands. 'Thank you . . . both of you.'

'*Prego*,' said Alberto.

'What's that mean?'

'Italian for don't mention it,' I said.

She laughed, a little unsteadily. 'I want to mention it over and over and over again . . . a thousand million times I want to mention it.'

'We are most happy to have been at your service,' said Alberto. His deep brown eyes regarded her with frank admiration.

'When I think what would have . . . ' She shivered.

'Then don't think about it,' I said. 'It's all over. You're safe.'

'Yes, I'm safe. But it isn't all over, is it?'

'For you it is.'

'I mean the whole mad business.'

'No, we weren't able to recover the loot or find out where it's gone or where this man who calls himself Juan Francesco is.'

She sat up in bed with her oval chin cupped in ringless hands. 'I went to Norfolk to see if I could get some background for an article about the art stealers,' she said. 'If I'd had even an inkling of what was involved . . . murder and violence . . . '

I lit a cigarette and said: 'That part's

unusual, it doesn't normally fit in with the racket. But something went wrong and they had to act. Who piloted the plane — Jiri?'

'Yes. Borge came with us. He said someone else would drive his car back into Thetford and then on to London.'

'Arkwright must have interrupted them and they killed him,' I said. 'Then you showed up and they had to take you with them. You'd seen them. How did that happen?'

'I drove out to the manor just on impulse. I thought I would introduce myself to Sir James and have a chat and get to know the value of the collection — all that sort of thing. I rang the bell and Borge opened the door and that was it.'

'He was wearing a nylon stocking mask when the butler answered the door.'

'Well, he didn't have it on when I arrived.'

'He must have taken it off and had no time to put it back when you rang. He couldn't leave it unanswered. So you saw his face and they bundled you into the plane when they left.'

'Yes.' She dropped her hand on mine and said: 'You came all the way from Norfolk to find me. That's something I'm never going to forget.'

'I had to do something. I realized they must have kidnapped you.' I grinned. 'At first Power — that's a police inspector who came over from Norwich — thought you were one of the gang.'

'*Well*!'

'It seemed reasonable, just at first. Apparently there's a woman art thief known as The Charmer who's been known to pose as a magazine writer.'

'How did you know I was genuine, then?'

I told her. She leaned forward suddenly and brushed her lips against my cheek. 'I'll spend all my life being grateful to you . . . Dale.'

Alberto chuckled. 'The *signorina* she like you very much,' he said.

'You, too, Alberto, for coming to that dreadful place with Dale.'

'I enjoy the trip,' replied Alberto. 'Do I not meet the most beautiful young

English girl?' He turned to me and added: 'What next, my good friend?'

'First, I think Linda had better get several hours' sleep.'

'I *am* tired,' she said. 'But how about you and Alberto?'

'Later. Meanwhile, I'd better contact the British Consulate and fix it for you to fly back to England with me.'

'Why not stay here for the agreeable summer holiday?' demanded Alberto.

'I'd like few things better, but I have to be back in England and it'd be as well if Linda didn't fly alone.'

Alberto sighed. '*Mi dispiace!*' He extended both arms in a gesture. 'What is to be must be. If you desire to use the telephone it is in the lounge.'

I used it, setting an appointment with a fellow who sounded like an Old Etonian newscaster. Alberto came out with a finger to his lips. 'The Signorina Linda she is asleep,' he said.

'She needs it.'

'*Si*. You have made the appointment?'

'Yes, in thirty minutes.' I yawned widely.

'You are tired, also Alberto. But I shall not nod the head in sleep. I shall stay by her side until your return. Is better, eh?'

'You don't expect these hoodlums to snatch her out of your apartment, do you?'

'Who can say? These men are dangerous. Perhaps they seek her in Milano.'

'How can they do that? They never even saw you.'

'Just the same, I stay by her side,' said Alberto.

I shaved, changed my shirt and walked. The fellow who had answered the phone was helpful — after I'd told him everything. There was no reason why I shouldn't. 'If you will bring Miss Travers along all will be in order,' he said.

'She's catching-up on some sleep — suppose we say after lunch, around two-thirty?'

'Excellent.'

'By the way, what did Logan say about me when you called him in London?'

'Various things,' he said urbanely.

I went out into the sun-drenched

streets. Milan is the commercial heart of Italy, lacking Rome's awesome evocation of the past; preoccupied, almost in an American sense, with material progress — though the unique cathedral in its vast square restores something of the cultural balance. But I was too tired to stand and look. I went back to the apartment and stretched out on one of the two settees, Alberto on the other. I awoke with a small start. Linda Travers was bending over me. She looked stunning.

'I've taken a shower and put on a new face but the same old clothes,' she said. 'Come on, up you get — you too Alberto. It's high noon.'

We ate in a *ristorante* below sidewalk level in a block facing the cathedral. I got flight tickets on a BEA Viscount taking off for London at five o'clock. At 2.29 we presented ourselves to the Old Etonian. Everything was in readiness.

When we left we strolled into the main shopping arcade because Linda wanted to buy something Italian to take back with her. It suddenly struck me that I had never been shopping with a woman before; one of the minor experiences of life I've missed. Or avoided.

She aimed a finger at a tan-coloured jersey suit elegantly set out on the polished floor behind a plateglass window. 'That's for me,' she announced. 'It's exactly right. Don't you boys think so?'

'Yeah,' I said.

'*Bella!*' cried Alberto. He flashed a dazzling smile. 'For you, Linda, this has been specially designed by an angel. I shall buy it for you myself, as a parting gift.'

She laughed. 'I can't let you do that, Alberto.'

'Why not?'

'I don't know — except that I can't go around accepting presents from men.'

'Not from men — just from Alberto, your devoted admirer.'

'It's lovely of you but, truly, I can't let you do it,' she said firmly.

'The English they are so — how you say it? — puritan,' sighed Alberto. 'You will, however, permit me to accompany you into the store?'

'Yes, you can do that.' She led the way in.

Alberto touched my arm. 'What is wrong with my buying Linda the small gift?' he demanded.

'It suggests a romantic attachment,' I grinned.

'I like the suggestion very much.' He made a magnificent shrug. 'But it is not to be. For you, though, perhaps.'

'You must be joking.'

'She glances at you once or twice when you are not observing, my friend. I think she like you a little.'

'A little isn't enough to start something, for Pete's sake.'

'For Alberto it would be more than enough. Then I make the little into much — like that!' He snapped his fingers.

We walked out of the arcade and across the *piazza* — three abreast, Linda in the middle. A deferential youngish fellow swung a reflex camera and said: '*Scusi, signorina, signore.*'

I started to say something in English. He smiled. '*Inglese*, eh? Perhaps you permit me to photograph just the *signorina?* For the magazine I represent.'

'Well . . . if she doesn't mind . . . '

Linda laughed. 'Why not? I've never had my *picture* in a magazine!'

She stepped into temporary isolation. He took his picture, then said: 'One more, *signorina* — over here.'

She moved forward, almost to the sidewalk edge. The door of a shabby black car opened suddenly. A long arm came out and jerked her sprawling inside. The youngish fellow wheeled on us. The camera was hanging down his chest on the straps and a long silenced gun was in his hand.

'*Grazie tante, signore,*' he said. He went backwards. The car was already moving when he jumped in.

Then it was going fast through the traffic.

10

Alberto's car was about twenty-five yards away. We raced for it, neither of us speaking. Alberto gunned the motor and shot across the square on an upward surge of gear shifts. The shabby black car was going south with a useful start, but we could see it going through traffic lights at an intersection. The lights changed to red as we reached them, but we went through too.

A big truck rumbled out of a side street, straddling the road. This time we had to stop. When we nosed round the back of it the car was far in the distance.

'They must be making for the *autostrada*,' shouted Alberto.

I didn't answer. There wasn't anything to say. I guessed that Borge or Jiri had spotted me in Milan and sent the car to pick Linda up, choosing their time. I sat rigidly forward in the bucket seat, staring through the glass. The black car swept round a bend, out of sight. It was a 1500 Volkswagen, not specially fast — but fast enough when you have a head start.

'I've got its number,' said Alberto.

The traffic thickened. We had to slow down — and the German car disappeared altogether. If Alberto was right we could catch up with it on the motorway. If he was wrong we had lost it. I could feel my fingernails biting into my palms.

We reached the terminal toll-gate on the Highway of the Sun, the start of the four hundred and seventy-two miles of twin double-track carriageway which slashes straight down the middle of Italy to Naples and cost more than £156,000,000 to build.

Alberto poked his head through the wound-down window and spoke rapidly in Italian. He took off in second, turned and said: 'We're on the right route, *amico* — a black Volkswagen went through the toll five minutes ago.'

He trod violently on the accelerator. I watched the needle shooting up through the sixties and seventies into the high eighties. We were streaking through the lush plains of Lombardy. Piacenza lay ahead, an exquisite town with rose-red battlements glowing in the sun, but I scarcely saw it or the great bridge over the valley of the River Po which carries the *autostrada* on its headlong flight south-eastward to Cortemaggiore and Parma.

I looked down at the clock again. The needle was rock-steady at ninety-five. At this speed we must catch-up within minutes. But the minutes sped by and still no sign of the Volkswagen.

Above the roar of the wind I yelled: 'They must have turned off!'

'*Si.*' He took his foot off the pedal. 'There are two exits near Parma — south-west for La Spezia, north-east for Mantua. What do we do?'

I thought rapidly. 'I've a hunch they won't be going east, Alberto.'

'Okay.' He came right down, cruising into the slipway. We hit the branch road and a sign loomed: *Passaggio a livello.* A railroad level-crossing. Lights flashed and the barrier arm descended. A long train thundered past. It seemed like minutes, sitting there watching it.

Beyond the crossing and round the bend we linked-up with the road for La Spezia. Alberto pulled into a service station and climbed out. The attendant speared a finger down the roadway.

Alberto came back, grinning. 'You have the good hunch, Dale,' he said. 'They stopped here long enough to buy a can of *benzina*, put it in the boot and went on again.'

'How long since?'

'Six or seven minutes. I now drive most fast.'

The road ran almost straight, due west for the Mediterranean coastline. But there would be junctions — for La Spezia, Rappallo, Genoa. We had to sight the Volkswagen first.

Then, suddenly, we saw it — a black blob on a distant rise. Alberto hurled the Fiat down the incline and we went up the opposite slope in the seventies. When we reached the summit the road ran straight again, as far as the eye could reach. It was empty . . .

I yelled: 'Stop the car!'

He came down through the gears,

pumping the brake pedal. The car came to a halt between high grassy banks.

'They've turned off,' I said.

Alberto shaded his eyes, staring ahead. 'There is no intersection, *amico*, nowhere for them to turn.'

'They must have.' I got out. Fifty yards ahead a rickety gate swung open on creaking hinges. I took the gun out and ran toward it. I could hear Alberto close behind. I slowed to a walk as we came near.

'You think they have run the car into the field?' he breathed.

'I don't know, we'll find out. Keep to the side and duck as we get close up.'

We reached the end of the grassy bank. The gate was only yards ahead. Far in the distance a farm truck growled into motion. There was no other sound. I got down flat on my stomach and poked my head round the gatepost. The German car was inside the field, not more than twenty paces away. A man was crouched on one side of it with a rifle. I couldn't see anybody else. An alarm signal went off inside me, but I still had to do something.

I whispered: 'Tell him he's covered, Alberto.'

He nodded, and shouted in Italian.

There was a small silence, then a spear of orange flame and the high whine of a bullet. I put the gun round the gate and triggered it, but he had gone down flat on the ground.

Alberto picked up a heavy stone. 'I divert his attention and you try again.'

'All right.'

He swung the stone in his right hand, came up fast and flung it. Even before it hit the car there was a rapid series of blasts from another section of the field, then a scurry of footsteps. I jerked my head sideways. It gave them the time they wanted. The man with the rifle was behind the wheel again and the youngish fellow with the camera dived in alongside him. The youngish one was firing a sub-machine gun, spraying bullets wildly.

But one hit Alberto. He spun completely round, then slumped into me. The impact threw me into a narrow ditch. When I crawled out the Volkswagen had gone and Alberto was trying to stop the blood spurting from his left forearm. The bullet was still in it. I tore a long strip off my shirt and made a bandage, tight. He gasped: 'The car . . . '

I ran back to it. Part of one of the tyres was ripped to shreds. It would take minutes to change the wheel and by that time we would have completely lost the Volkswagen.

Alberto had already opened the boot and dragged the jack out with one hand. I made the change. Neither of us spoke while I did it.

Finally, Alberto said: 'We cannot hope to catch them now.'

'We've got to try.'

'*Si*, we try. You will have to drive, my friend.'

'Yes, to the nearest doctor.'

'There is not the time.'

'You'll have to see one. We can't leave it.'

'The *signorina* was in the car, I saw her.'

'I just caught a glimpse from the ditch. She was shouting something or other . . . ' I stopped.

Alberto said: 'You have thought of something?'

I didn't answer. I ran back to the gate and went through it, and on to the flattened grass where the Volkswagen had stood. Nothing. It was too much to hope that there would be. But I started rummaging around in the grass just the same. The faint chance, the one you try when everything else seems lost. Nothing but the flattened grass and the ruts made in it by the tyres. I stood in the middle of it, defeated.

The wind, warm and scented, lifted my hair. I followed its direction, walking diagonally from where the car had stood. I looked up toward the bank and the hedgerow jutting above it. Something small and white was lodged there. I reached for it.

It was an envelope with words scrawled on it: *Sestri Levante — Linda*.

I went back to the car and started driving. Ten miles later we came to a village and I found the local doctor and he said Alberto had a minor fracture and needed hospital treatment to get the slug out.

'We have to press on, it is of the utmost

urgency, *dottore*,' Alberto objected.

The doctor smiled without humour. 'If you continue without the treatment you may have the gangrene, *signor*.'

'You'll have to get it done, old chum,' I said.

'God damn everything!' said Alberto.

'I'm sorry, but . . . '

'*Si*, I understand.' He gripped my hand. 'You take the car and go on alone, immediately.'

The doctor said: 'I will drive you to the hospital. Your friend can telephone there later.'

'I'll do that,' I said.

'*Arrivederci*, my good and dear friend,' said Alberto.

I took the through route to Sestri Levante. On the fringe of the little resort I saw the Volkswagen — abandoned. They must have switched cars.

It was almost dark when I drove on to the tree-lined promenade. Maybe they were no more than a few hundred yards from me, but it might as well be a thousand miles because now I couldn't even tell anyone what car I was looking for . . .

11

Multi-coloured lights nodded in the tall palms and under the trees vacation visitors strolled without hurry, talking in half a dozen tongues. I parked opposite the Grand Villa Balbi Hotel and got out. A tall man wearing a fine suntan and greying hair came through the doorway smoking a pipe with a wide bowl. He took the pipe from between his teeth and called over his shoulder: 'Ready, darling?'

An Englishman. Maybe he could tell me nothing, but I could try. I didn't know enough Italian to get beyond a dozen routine phrases, which is worse than knowing nothing because it invites a reply in a flood of idiomatic native language.

I said: 'I'm an American — I wonder if you'd mind talking with me for a moment.'

He gave me an alert eye. 'You're not trying to make a touch, are you?'

'No.'

'I didn't really think you were, you don't look like a con man,' he said amiably. 'Not that I'm quite certain how a con man is supposed to look.'

'Like anybody else, I guess, but I'm not one. The name is Shand, Dale Shand.'

'Charles Lockwood.' He held out a fine brown hand. 'What can I do for you, Mr. Shand?'

'I'm not sure that you can do anything. It's just a chance. I'm trying to trace three people, two men and a girl, who arrived in Sestri Levante within the last half-hour.'

He smiled. 'Friends of yours and you've mislaid them, eh?'

'It's not quite like that. I . . . '

A woman came out of the hotel; about fifty, very well-dressed. 'Oh, Charles, I'll have to run up to our room again, I've forgotten something.' She saw me for the first time and looked inquiringly.

Lockwood said: 'This is Mr. Dale Shand, an American. Wants to ask me something.'

'How do you do, Mrs. Lockwood?' I said.

She made a pleasant smile. 'You two have your chat while I run upstairs. I shan't be long.'

'I think,' said Lockwood urbanely, 'I think you had better look for us in the bar when you come down.'

'The same thought had already occurred to me,' said his wife, without malice.

We went in and I ordered two Scotches and said: 'This will seem damned odd to you, Mr. Lockwood. I can only ask you to believe me when I say it happens to be a matter of extreme urgency.'

He paused with his glass half-way to his lean mouth. 'Good Lord, old boy,' he said in a startled voice. 'You *are* being serious?'

'Yeah — very.' I didn't hesitate. I told him the whole outline. What was there to lose? He heard me out, finished his drink and called for two more.

I said: 'The car Miss Travers was taken away in was ditched less than a mile from here. They must have been met by another. I have no means whatever of identifying it, but there's just a chance that you may have seen two men and a girl go past in one. The girl is almost certainly in the rear of the car and no less certainly would look frightened.'

The mess-jacketed waiter came up with the drinks, accepted a fifty-lire tip and drifted away. Lockwood said: 'I'm sorry, I haven't noticed anything. But, then, I wouldn't. I was probably in the bath when they passed here — if they came this way.'

I sat there, without words, my drink untasted like his.

'Look here, old boy,' said Lockwood, 'hadn't you better get in touch with the local bobbies?'

'The police?'

'If this young lady has been abducted . . .' he began.

I said: 'I was trying to get an immediate lead. But I guess it was too much to hope for.'

His wife came in with a swish of satin. She must have been a stunner in her thirties and still looked better than good. I stood up to go. She eyed the table in mild surprise. 'Aren't you stopping to have your drink, Mr. Shand?'

'No, I'm sorry — I just haven't the time.'

Lockwood said impassively: 'Mr. Shand is trying to find two fellows who have kidnapped a young English girl. He wondered if by some slight chance I'd seen them driving past the hotel and . . . what on earth's the matter, Mary?'

She was staring fixedly at me. Then she made a small movement. 'Oh, it's too ridiculous. I'm letting my imagination run away with me . . . '

I said urgently: 'If you saw anything — anything at all — please tell me what it was.'

'Well, Charles was taking a bath and I was making my face up. I happened to glance down at the promenade and saw a large white car go past. There were three men in it, the driver and two others. One was with a girl in the back. I thought she looked ill or something. Then, as it went past, the man turned to her and said something. I couldn't hear what he said, of course — but she seemed to, well, sort of shrink back.'

I could hear my own breathing, like a

137

hard rustle of sound. 'Which way did it go?'

'Just down the front, toward the harbour.'

'You said it was a large white car, Mrs. Lockwood. Do you happen to know what make?'

'I don't really know much about cars. I can never remember the number of ours, though we've had it several years. I'm sorry . . . ' She broke off and added: 'Wait a minute, I *did* notice one thing — the rear number plate was loose. I mean it was hanging down a little at one side — you know, as if the car had been accidentally backed into something.'

I picked up my drink and swallowed it in one.

'Have I helped you, Mr. Shand?' she asked.

'Very much so. Perhaps a great deal more than you know.'

Lockwood set fire to his vast pipe again. 'Look here, d'you want a bit of help?' he said. 'I'm not so young as I was, but I was a major of Commandos in the last war and . . . '

'Thanks, but I can't involve you in this, Mr. Lockwood.'

'What are you going to do?'

'Find the car first.'

'And then call the local police, eh?'

'Something like that,' I lied.

I got back in the car and drove down to the harbour. It made a long jutting arm from the shore. Scores of small craft were moored close in. Further out speedboats were still skimming across the water, shining like a blue-black mirror under the reflected light from the promenade. Cars were parked sideways along the harbour. I left mine and walked past them, carefully and one by one. I counted five Alfa-Romeos, three Renaults, a Mercedes, a couple of British makes — a Humber Sceptre and a Cambridge, both very new — and four Simcas. No large white car with or without a dislodged number plate.

I walked on. I was near the top of the harbour when I saw it, a white Ford Zodiac parked in the shadows against a high wall on my left. The rear of the car was almost touching the wall. There was no one in it. I went round the back and looked down, one hand splayed on the boot. The number plate was almost half off. It was a French registration.

The doors and windows were locked. I looked inside, but there was nothing on the seats or the shelf. Where had they gone? They must be near. I looked at the high wall. Above it was a place which looked like a hotel. There were no houses anywhere near. A boat, perhaps a fast cruiser? I walked across the harbour and looked down at the water. There were at least a dozen cruisers tied-up.

A man with a face like a pickled walnut was leaning over the low wall. He was wearing a navy blue jersey and a peaked cap.

I said haltingly: '*Buona sera, signor. Mi trovo in difficotta. Il Signor Juan Francesco abita qui?*'

The fisherman pointed a finger at the bay. 'Over there, *signor*.'

'*Parla inglese?*'

'*Si*, a little. You wish to contact him, eh?'

'You mean he has a house across the bay?'

He shook his head. 'You not onnerstan' — I mean the boat, the big one out there, *signor*.'

I had seen it, but it hadn't meant anything until now. It was a big powered yacht rising impressively from the water and probably painted white if you saw it close up. I was going to. 'You have a boat yourself?' I asked.

He pointed again, down at the water just below us. A small cabin cruiser was rocking gently on it. 'You wish me to take you out to the yacht?'

I nodded.

'Two t'ousand lire, *signor*. If you desire me to wait and bring you back, another two t'ousand.'

It seemed a stiffish charge for a taxi ride of less than a quarter-mile, but I'd have paid double if he'd asked it.

We were midway there when he said: 'The rich *signor* go out to the yacht with several others, but they return, except the young *signorina*.'

'Then there's just him and the crew?'

'No, the crew is not yet on board — later they come. Another hour, I

141

theenk. They are enjoying themselves in the town. You will be company for the *signor*, no doubt he will be most glad to see you.'

Well, Señor Juan Francesco, alias El Rapier, was going to meet one crewman he wasn't expecting. It seemed improbable that he would be glad.

We came alongside. Close up, it was a handsome white-painted yacht flying the French flag and a rope ladder hung down the side. I started up it, looked down and said: 'Wait for me.'

'How long?'

'About ten minutes if I'm lucky.' His leathery face stared up in perplexity.

I dropped without sound on to the deck, walking slowly on the balls of my feet. I found the companionway and went down it, one step at a time. Light showed ahead of me. A short corridor led off to the right. A door was ajar. I guessed it opened on the lounge or dining cabin. From beyond the door I heard a faint scraping. I sniffed at the air. Cigar smoke from Ramon Allones.

I stood close up to the door. A man's

voice, deep but not mellow; a voice with a hard edge to it. He said something in Spanish, then immediately switched to English — flawlessly and with the inflexions of an upper-class Englishman. Maybe he was an Oxford don as well as a Spanish one?

'We sail as soon as the crew are all on board . . . ' A pause, then: 'It is a pity the troublesome Mr. Shand is still at large.'

I supposed he was talking to Linda Travers — but not for long. The voice which answered him was a woman's, not one I had ever heard before.

'Yes, our American friend seems to have been too clever for you, Juan.' There was a hint of mockery in the words.

'You find it amusing, my dear Carmen?'

'Not necessarily — I merely stated what seems to be beyond dispute.'

There was another silence. I wondered who she was. She must have already been on the yacht. The boatman's description of the young *signorina* fitted Linda. He hadn't mentioned another girl. A woman with a Spanish name, though she sounded English. But so did Francesco.

He said slowly: 'Borge and Jiri managed to reach the Italian side of the lake after Shand blew up the petrol cans. Fortunately, they had money on them — enough to get to Milan and arrange for the re-possession of Miss Travers. To that extent Shand has not been too clever for us. It is essential that she does not impart her knowledge to the authorities.'

Carmen laughed. 'Well, there is a lot of water between here and England.'

'Quite. When we reach the sceptr'd isle she will not be among those who step buoyantly ashore.'

'Shand also has knowledge.'

'Some, not enough — Miss Travers, on the other hand, actually witnessed incidents at Grange Manor.'

'Just the same, it would be better if Shand were also at the bottom of the deep blue sea, wouldn't you say?'

'Naturally, but we do not know exactly where he is.'

'No doubt he will show himself in due course, if not here then in England. What then?'

'My dear Carmen, what an unnecessary question!'

'Perhaps, perhaps not. Getting rid of Shand may not be easy.'

'You think he is too smart for us, do you?'

'I didn't say that — but you must admit that he's done rather well so far.'

'I do not underrate him, my sweet — but, after all, we have Miss Travers. I agree that he seems to be a man of persistence and resource. It will be a pleasure to meet him, though it is a pleasure he will not share.'

'You mean to kill him?'

'But, of course. Such men are dangerous.' Francesco made a curious laugh. 'That will be the ultimate pleasure — one which I shall not hurry over.'

'Oh . . . '

'You find the idea disagreeable?' he purred.

'If you want to know, yes.'

'The fastidious young English miss, eh?'

'You don't have to sneer, Juan. I recognize the necessity of removing

Shand, but not what you're proposing.'

The Spaniard's voice suddenly lost its schooled urbanity. 'Shand has caused me too much trouble — for that he shall pay. I propose to introduce him to the meticulously calculated refinements of the Inquisition.'

'You've got to find him first.'

'He will appear, of that I am certain. And this time we shall be ready for him.'

'Why kill him at all?'

'You are, of course, joking, my sweet. It is an imperative necessity. Or have you something else to suggest?'

'Yes. I think Shand would be a useful member of our organization. Infinitely better than either Borge or Jiri.'

'My God,' he said, 'you have a point. I hadn't considered that.'

'Unless you hate him so much that you can't resist the temptation to kill him.'

'The temptation is strong, but I can resist it if necessary. You open up an interesting avenue of thought. A resolute man able to act on his own initiative in totally unexpected crises . . . yes, such a man would be most valuable to us.'

'Assuming, of course, that he is not incorruptible.'

'That can readily be ascertained when we meet, as assuredly we shall. Well, it's something to think about. Meanwhile, we dispose of the girl.'

'When?'

'Soon. Once we are safely at sea. She has also caused us much trouble, but to her I shall be merciful — a quick exit. By the way, where have you put her?'

'In the small cabin down the corridor.'

I went there. The key was in the lock. I turned it. A small cry came from inside. I pushed the door open and held a finger up to my mouth. She was standing close to a bunk in a small carpeted room whose only furniture was a circular table and a hard-backed chair.

'Don't speak, Linda. Just come with me — we're getting out of here.'

She nodded dumbly. I took her arm, walking her across the carpet and out into the passage. We were almost level with the main cabin when the door opened and a woman with long ash blonde hair and wearing an Italian two-piece stepped out, straight into us.

She opened her mouth to yell. I clapped a hand over it, pushing her head back. Her teeth bit into me. She twisted free, enough to scream: '*Juan* . . . '

I slammed her against the wall of the passage as he came through the doorway. He was tall, about my height, but broader. His face was slightly heavy, neither handsome nor ugly, the kind of slightly heavy face you can see on a lot of men. His right eye seemed to be lazy, off dead centre. He pulled up, standing with his legs apart.

'To paraphrase a historic greeting — Mr. Shand, I presume?' he said.

His good eye darted at the blonde and I made the tactical error of looking. A split second of time, but it was enough. Something long and steely had jumped into his hand. A swordstick — and now he had the rapier unsheathed.

It stabbed the air as I stepped sideways and dived for his legs. He leaped backwards into the cabin. My hands clawed at his knees and we hit the floor together, going down in a tangled mass.

I could see the blonde in the doorway. She had a .25 automatic out, but she couldn't shoot it and be certain of not hitting the Spaniard. If we broke apart she could, though. We rolled over and over, alternately on top and under each other. Francesco's hand rammed my chin up. I gave him a knee and he screeched, toppling back.

The blonde could shoot now, but she didn't. Instead, she banged down on the floor in a flurry of skirts. Linda Travers leaned against the inside of the door with a flower vase in her hand.

My own gun was on the floor and Francesco was back on his feet with the rapier. I knocked the blade sideways before he could lunge with it.

The Spaniard laughed. He darted at an angle across the confined space, pirouetting like a ballet dancer, then swept in with the sword straight out. I was trapped on the end of it, the tip against my throat.

He used the merest pressure. The steel just pricked my flesh. I could feel the small, short pain, like a wasp sting. Then, slowly, he took the rapier back, no more than inches.

'Sudden death is too good for you, Mr. Shand . . . I shall order other arrangements.' Without turning, he added: 'For your would-be rescuer's immediate sake, do not make any ill-timed move, Miss Travers.'

He smiled, a long brilliant smile full of nothing. 'Gonzales will be here soon, Mr. Shand. It will be his task to introduce you to the contemporary mysteries of the revived Inquisition . . . '

12

We were in a space below the water-line; a small dark space like a ship's hold in miniature. The clogged air had an oily reek.

I put out a hand. It touched her body, cold and shaking.

'Dale . . . ' Her voice was a dry sob.

I moved, wound an arm round her, holding her against me to stop the trembling. 'We're not done yet,' I said. The words sounded hollow, meaningless.

She clung to me, her face buried in my chest. 'Oh, God — it's like a nightmare!'

I stood there with her. Minutes passed. My eyes adjusted enough to see dimly. Objects swam into focus, shaping themselves into stacked crates, lengths of ship's rope, a rough bench, an open oil drum. That was where the reek was coming from.

She had stopped shivering. 'I seem to do nothing except get you into trouble,' she whispered. 'And . . . and I thought at first that . . . '

'I know, you thought I was one of them.'

'I'm sorry.'

'It doesn't matter. There's only one thing now — somehow, we have to get out of here before Gonzales, whoever he is, shows. Or be ready for him.'

The shiver ran through her again. 'They're going to . . . '

'Yeah, that's what we have to beat.'

I went across the floor, still holding her. The door was locked. What else? But soon men would come through it, men with guns. I had — how long? Ten minutes, maybe more. But in the end they would come and I had to be ready. I could stand to the side of the door and chop one of them down, but the others would get me.

There was a small iron grille let in the door. The panel behind it opened and Francesco's face appeared.

'The crew are on their way, Mr. Shand — I thought you would like to know. They will be here very shortly. Perhaps you will care to hear what will be prepared for you?'

I said nothing because there wasn't anything, not now. Perhaps not at any time.

Francesco smiled. 'Gonzales will take charge of you, Mr. Shand. I should explain that he is a torturer of exquisite skill and unimaginable resource and at one time practised his art in Algiers. His speciality is in the thoughtful application of ingenious electrical devices to the human body . . . you do not seem suitably afraid, *amigo*.'

He was wrong, but I went on saying nothing.

The Spaniard pressed his face up against the grille. 'The room in which you will be able personally to judge the limitless extent of Gonzales's rare skills is just beyond the small corridor in which I am standing. You will be conducted there immediately the crew come aboard, which will be in not more than seven minutes from now. I leave you in contemplation . . . '

The panel slid back. A small choked

cry came from Linda. I didn't answer. I had to do something, anything. I tried to wrench a slat from one of the crates; it would make some kind of weapon. But the crate was as solid as a strong-box. Given time I might have made it, but they weren't going to give me any time.

I breathed in through my mouth. The reek seemed stronger. Something stirred in my mind, making an idea. I turned, almost knocking a drum over. I grabbed it, but not before black shining oil seeped over the rim. It started oozing over the floor and I almost slipped on it.

Linda was struggling to speak, but I wasn't listening. I said: 'Get behind me, against the wall. Don't say anything — just do it.'

'All right . . . '

I tipped the big drum right over. The oil surged out like a thick black lake. I tilted another, across where the door would open, and stepped back against the wall. We stood without movement, almost without breathing. I could hear the distant plop of water against the side of the yacht, nothing else. For minutes there was nothing else. Then I heard it — the thud of booted feet. Every nerve in my body felt strung out, taut to the point of snapping.

The door opened. A man came through it. He had a sub-machine gun in the crook of his arm. But not for long.

His feet slid right out from under him and he shot straight across the black ooze on his back with his legs outspread. He slammed into the opposite wall, bounced off and his head hit a crate and he rolled over and was still. I could have done with his machine gun, but it was embalmed in oil.

'Quick,' I breathed. I thrust her through the door ahead of me, closed it and turned the key in the lock. The passage was short, a small connecting passage between two rooms. Gonzales was in the other one. The door wasn't fully closed, so I could see him. A tall gangling man with jet-black hair and overlong sideburns down a pock-marked face with a nose like an eagle's beak.

He was making terminal adjustments to a steel cabinet, fitting flex to small, curiously-designed objects. The cabinet had a frontal panel with circular controls. Señor Gonzales preparing the delicate instruments of persuasion. He stood back from the cabinet, surveying it with delight. He pranced sideways to a single lever positioned in the wall, but didn't throw it. Not yet. It wasn't the time.

I poked the door with an index finger, another inch. He was back facing the cabinet. A deep chuckle welled from him.

'Bring Señor Shand in, *amigo* . . . .' He spoke over his shoulder. His back was still turned. He was holding the flex again, in both hands.

I kicked the door wide open and jumped in — not at Gonzales. He heard me, but not fast enough. I hit the lever full down. There was a blinding flash, white as a laser ray. A continuous scream came from him, like a thin tormented nerve in an endless crescendo. His entire body contorted. The live terminals were still in his hands, as if welded to them. I knocked the lever up and he staggered back, free of the current but with both hands like obscene fingers of blackened toast.

He ran round and round the room, screaming and sobbing. Linda was out in the corridor. I stood in the doorway, blocking her view. A laugh sounded above us. Then a voice. Francesco's voice, calling in Spanish: 'Already Señor Shand is in the hot embrace, eh . . . this I must savour . . . '

Footsteps, but still at a distance. I pushed Linda down the passage. There was a narrow companion-way. Suppose we met El Rapier coming down? I grinned wolfishly.

But we were there first, on the deck and racing across it. The small cruiser was still rocking gently on the water — the yacht crew must have approached from the other side.

There was just time. Shouts belched from below deck. They had found Gonzales.

Linda went down the rope ladder first, swaying — but she made it. I swung myself over the side, dropped the last five feet into the cruiser.

The fisherman said: '*Che cosa è successo?*'

'Never mind what's happened — get the hell out of here if you want to go on living,' I said.

'*Si, signor* — we go!'

We were half-way to the harbour when figures showed darkly on the yacht's deck. Nobody fired any shots, though. Before we came alongside the harbour wall a dull throbbing sounded and in another moment the yacht was putting out to sea.

★ ★ ★

I got the car and started driving. Linda sat rigid, staring through the windscreen, not speaking. I touched her clasped hands. On a hot summer night they were zero cold. I stopped the car outside the hotel and took her into the bar and ordered Italian *cognac*, two powerful ones.

'I don't like brandy,' she said.

'Drink your nice medicine,' I directed.

'Yes, Dr. Shand, if you say so.'

'You need it. I need it myself, if it comes to that.'

'Yes,' she said. 'What did you do to that man, Gonzales?'

'He was holding some electrical devices and I switched the current on for a few seconds.'

'Oh!'

'He won't be able to use his hands for some time. I guess I did it without even thinking.'

She looked directly at me. 'You don't have to apologize,' she said.

'No.'

'Just the same, what you did was out of character.'

'How's that?'

'I think you're a kind of civilized man,' she answered simply.

'Thanks. As I say, I didn't stop to think, but there was probably an unformulated motive — the realization of what he must have done to a lot of helpless guys.'

'Yes. You gave him a taste of his own medicine. But it's nothing to what he would have done to you.'

Time passed. It didn't matter. Francesco

was far out in the Mediterranean. I could go to the police, but long before I'd finished explaining the yacht would be outside territorial waters, heading — where?

Lockwood strolled into the bar. 'Good Lord — you back already, old boy?'

I nodded.

'So you were able to rescue the young lady?' His eyes rested on Linda with open admiration.

'Miss Travers — Mr. Lockwood,' I said.

'How do you do, Mr. Lockwood?' murmured Linda.

'I say, you look deuced upset . . . '

'Miss Travers has had a somewhat trying time, but she's all right now.'

'Good show.' He eyed me shrewdly. 'I have an idea that you helped this charming young lady alone and unaided, Shand.'

'As a matter of fact, yes.'

'Didn't call in the local bobbies after all?'

'There wasn't time.'

'But if there's been dirty work at the crossroads oughtn't they to be informed, old boy?'

'It doesn't matter now, does it?'

'No, I suppose not. Especially if you don't know the lingo. What exactly happened?'

'Miss Travers was being held against her will on a yacht. I was lucky enough to get her off it.'

Linda put an arm through mine, holding it tight against her. 'It wasn't luck, Mr. Lockwood. It was a lot of courage and some very fast thinking.'

Lockwood said quietly: 'I rather think you're a man after my own heart, Shand. Wish I'd been with you . . . '

A voice called from the doorway: 'Charles — our friends have arrived, we're waiting for you.'

'Yes, dear,' said the ex-Commando dutifully.

He went away and Linda smiled at last. 'See what happens when you're well and truly married,' she said.

We finished the brandies and I wedged myself in a telephone booth and called the operator: '*La signorina?*'

'*Si, signor.*'

I used some lame Italian to ask for the

continental service.

She said: 'Certainly, sir. I speak English.'

I told her what I wanted. She said there would be a thirty-minute delay. I bought two more drinks, less powerful this time. The call came through in twenty-five minutes.

Logan listened to what I had to tell him, then said: 'So the yacht got away?'

'Yeah — and don't tell me I've made a balls of everything.'

'I wasn't going to.'

I said: 'This man Francesco — what do you know about him?'

'Nothing. We'll try to find out.' He made a small, dry chuckle. 'You've done rather well, Shand. Too much to expect you to stop the yacht sailing. What are you doing next?'

'Flying back to England very shortly.'

'Excellent. Come straight to the Yard.'

'I managed to rescue Miss Travers,' I said. 'That's enough, so far as I'm concerned.'

'But not enough for us,' answered Logan imperturbably. 'You're not through yet, Shand.'

13

We drove out of Sestri Levante, picked Alberto up at the hospital and took him back to Milan, up through Parma and on to the *autostrada*.

'So I miss all the fun,' he sighed.

'You wouldn't have thought it funny if you'd been with us in that dreadful black hole on the yacht,' said Linda.

'*Mi dispiace, signorina,*' replied Alberto. 'I merely wish that I myself had been there to rescue you,' he added in English.

'I'm sure you have been most helpful, Alberto,' said Linda prettily.

'Instead, I fret and fume in the hospital while my good friend Dale steals all the limelight,' grinned Alberto. 'Always I am the unlucky one.'

Linda glanced round the handsome apartment. 'Not altogether unlucky . . . '

'I do not mean the material possessions, I refer to the honour of aiding a beautiful young Miss in her time of distress,' said Alberto gallantly. He made another enormous sigh. 'And now I suppose you leave me, eh?'

'We have to be back in London,' I said. 'The police want to talk to me.'

'That I can most readily comprehend.' He put his head a little to one side. 'But when the po-lice desire speech with the *investigatore privato* it is not always a prospect to relish.'

'Perhaps not. On the other hand, I can't very well refuse.'

'It would not be advisable, no. But you do not have to be in the great hurry. You will stay the night with me and catch the early flight in the morning, eh?'

'I want to be at New Scotland Yard by noon.'

'The flight arrive at London Airport at ten forty-five. It will be adequate.'

'All right.'

Linda said: 'How many bedrooms have you got here?'

'Two.' He grinned. 'One for me and one for . . . '

She coloured slightly. I said: 'I'll sleep on the settee.'

His good arm waved magnificently. '*Mama mia*, such reticence!'

'Alberto, you're incorrigible,' said Linda severely.

'Incor — what is that?'

'Awful, then.'

'*Che cosa ho fatto?*' cried Alberto.

'You've made an indelicate suggestion,' I said.

'You do not wish to be close together?' His handsome face registered astonishment. 'Ah, well — the ways of the English are most odd.'

'I'm not English,' I said.

'Also the *americano*, then.' He changed the subject. 'More coffee, Linda?'

'Yes, I'd like another cup.'

It grew late. Linda went into one of the bedrooms. She came back, put her head round the door and said softly: 'Bless you both.'

Alberto put blankets and cushions on the settee. 'I sleep here,' he announced.

'No you don't. I'm not robbing you of your own bed, old friend. In you go . . . don't argue!'

'Okay.' He started across the room,

turned and said: 'Is better that you remain here, now I think of it.'

'How do you mean, it's better?'

He grinned. 'Who can tell that the *signorina* will not emerge in the silent watches of the night, eh?'

'Get along with you,' I said.

The door closed behind him. I lit a cigarette and sat on the edge of the settee, thinking. Where was the yacht and what was stashed away in it? Maybe a million dollars' worth of looted art. But I didn't know. I'd never heard of art stealers running private luxury yachts. Perhaps we were up against something new, something bigger? Another thought surfaced — who was the girl called Carmen? Despite the Spanish name she looked and sounded English. That fired another train of thought, but I couldn't be sure. I wondered what Logan wanted of me and decided that whatever it was I wasn't going to play along. But maybe I'd have to if I wanted to stay amicably in England? I yawned and stretched out on the settee. I reached out a hand and switched off the table lamp.

I slept. How long? Ten minutes, two hours? I didn't know. All I knew was that I was suddenly awake and aware of a soft movement in the room.

A figure leaned over me. I caught the faint scent of *arpege*. I didn't move, didn't open my eyes. Her face came down and her mouth touched mine and went away and still I did nothing.

Maybe Alberto was right . . .

★　★　★

Logan looked up from his desk as I tramped in. 'George Carruthers sends his regards,' he said.

'That's fine, just like old times,' I grunted. It was Carruthers who had put the squeeze on me to help his security squad block some international and illegal arms manipulations which linked with a case I was working at last summer. I remembered him well — from the jaunty grey moustache and the expensively careless clothes to the kind of English voice which some Americans find insufferably arrogant because of the unconscious assumption of superiority instilled at the kind of schools from which the British ruling class is still largely drawn, despite the egalitarian revolution. In fact, I found George Carruthers ruthless but likeable and we got on fine. But art stealing didn't seem to be a case he was likely to be concerned with. Logan's next words said as much.

'Carruthers isn't in on this, not his line of country. But he wishes to be remembered to you and hopes you will have a drink with him at his club when you're finished.'

'When I'm finished doing what?'

'Doing a little job for us, Shand,' replied Logan amiably.

'I only came to this country just over a year ago and that makes it twice you've dragged me in.'

Logan allowed his eyebrows to lift fractionally. 'My dear chap, you don't object, surely?'

'And if I do?'

'Wouldn't make any difference, we'd still ask you.'

'Or put the pressure on me.'

'Pressure?'

'Well, last time it was hinted that I might be sent back to New York on the next plane out.'

Logan chuckled. 'Just a remark, no more than that.'

'George Carruthers would have done it all right if I hadn't played along.'

'Well, take it that this time we're not sending you back on the next plane or any other plane, Shand. In fact, if you flatly refuse to come in with us there's nothing we can do about it.'

'You could make things tough for me in my work. A discreet word here and there and my sources of revenue mysteriously dry up.'

Logan engineered a shocked look; very good engineering, but I wasn't deceived. 'My dear Shand, as if we would do such a thing,' he murmured.

'Don't go simple on me,' I growled. 'You fellows could write a thesis on the gentle art of hidden persuasion.'

'Thanks, the tribute is much appreciated. Now let's have your story in detail, shall we?' He said it as though there was no question whatever of my joining them. Well, I guess there wasn't.

When I was through he said thoughtfully: 'This chap Francesco interests me.'

'Well, he seems to be the head man in the art-stealing ring you're after.'

'Yes, of course. I should have used the word perplexed.'

'I don't quite get that.'

'I mean we have no record whatever of any art stealer named Francesco.'

'Another name? He could have several.'

'Perhaps, but we have no information about a Spaniard.'

'He could be an Englishman masquerading as a Spaniard,' I said slowly.

'What makes you say that?'

'He speaks flawless English without any foreign inflexion.'

'That's interesting. Perhaps a Spaniard educated at Oxford or Cambridge, though?'

'I guess it's possible.'

'We'll make some inquiries. Trouble is there's probably been quite a number of Spaniards at one or more of the universities. Still, we may be able to narrow the field.'

'The yacht,' I said. 'Did you trace it?'

'You omitted to tell us its name.'

'I didn't see it. It wasn't painted on the side where I went aboard.'

'Well, we did our best. A large white yacht put into Marseilles and took some crated goods aboard. Labelled pottery. The yacht owner's name was given as Jules Delange, of 269 Rue de Colisee, Paris. By the time we were able to get the authorities interested the yacht had left for the Middle East and Delange had left Marseilles in a private car, a Ferrari, registration not observed. A young woman was with him. Several men left by less ostentatious transport. Also, when the yacht sailed there was some new crew.'

'Borge and Jiri, plus a man named Gonzales, who would have both hands bandaged — what about them?'

Logan shrugged. 'Nobody had any special reason to make notes or ask questions, so we don't have any information as to their whereabouts. There's something else, though.'

'Oh, what?'

'We checked on Delange with the Sûreté — the address exists but no such person lives there. Charming.'

'Very,' I assented drily.

'This fellow Delange or Francesco or whatever his real name is has simply disappeared. He could be in Rome or Berlin, New York or right here in London.'

'Well?'

'We mean to find him, Shand. In fact, we *must* find him. If he's not in Britain then the job goes to Interpol — with some direct personal co-operation from us.'

'That seems to let me out, doesn't it?'

Logan chuckled. 'You're too optimistic. What I have in mind is your joining Interpol as one of our representatives.'

'You're joking.'

'On the contrary, I'm being quite serious. You acted for Special Security in that arms business. We liked what you did, despite your engaging habit of taking an independent line. Or even because of it. There is also the fact that you can identify this Spaniard, which is vital. No reason why you shouldn't do as well as on the last occasion.'

'Only this time you haven't such readily available means of applying pressure.'

'No, security isn't involved and you're now established here professionally. We could probably think of some pressure-points, though. But we'd prefer not to. In any event, you'll not be called upon unless we have to bring Interpol into it. What do you say?'

I seemed to be getting deeper and deeper into something which was little of my business and none of the client's. On the other hand, the goodwill of New Scotland Yard isn't to be disregarded and I liked Logan.

'I'll come in,' I said shortly.

Logan held out a strong hand. 'Good man. You'll be in London, I take it?'

'Yes and no. I have to go down to Norfolk again, but I'll be back almost at once.'

'This chap Leffiney, you mean?'

'Yes, I have to see him.'

'Power will probably be glad of a chat while you're there — he's still in Thetford.' Logan eyed me for a moment and went on: 'Miss Travers has already gone back there, hasn't she?'

'Yeah — I saw her off. She's gone partly to round-out her magazine assignment and partly to see Power.'

'Naturally. She's a witness, not a direct witness of the murder, but still an important witness.'

'She says Borge boasted of killing Arkwright. The guy called Jiri piloted the plane they made their getaway in.'

'Useful.' A thoughtful expression moved on his face. 'She'd better have some police protection.'

'So I thought. I sent a note down with her for Power, about that.'

'Not that these chaps are likely to revisit the Thetford area. In any case, they now have no opportunity of preventing Miss Travers telling what she knows. Still, better be sure than sorry.'

I nodded and went out. It was early afternoon on a perfect summer's day. I wasn't sure how perfect everything else was.

I went straight to my Baker Street office and there was Nancy looking the way she always looks, which is at all times rather more than fetching. She put her head a little to one side, tapped her teeth with a ballpoint and said: 'Did you have a nice trip?'

'I don't know whether you've selected the right adjective, Nancy.'

'Well, you had some agreeable company, I gather.'

I had phoned Nancy from the airport and mentioned Linda and maybe that was a tactical mistake. Too late now.

'I went to Milan and Lugano primarily to get Miss Travers out of a tough situation,' I said. 'In the event, I got into a worse one.'

'You did?'

'Yeah.'

'I wish you would stop saying yes like that, Mr. Shand,' said Nancy censoriously.

'I'm sorry.'

'What sort of tough spot were you in?'

I told her then — all of it. She shivered. 'Torture — in these days.'

'It happens. The great technological revolution hasn't changed the baser habits of men.'

'Some men,' she corrected.

'I meant some men. Scientific progress has merely placed nastier and even more efficient means in their hands. However, I beat them this time.'

Nancy's eyes widened in alarm. 'You aren't expecting *another* meeting with these dreadful persons, surely?'

'I'm not sure what I'm expecting. I'm just keeping my eyes open and my powder dry.'

'You don't carry a gun, not here in England.'

'I picked up one somewhere along the line and got it through Customs.'

'Meaning you smuggled it in?'

'That's right,' I replied cheerfully. 'Well, what's cooking?'

'Mr. Leffiney rang up from New York at one-fifteen p.m. He sounded somewhat irritable. He's calling you back at four — that is, in three minutes from now.'

I fingered rubbed-out flake into my pipe, set fire to it and stood chatting with Nancy. It occurred to me, not for the first time, that this comes under the heading of one of the more relaxing and agreeable things to do with one's time. Why don't I ask her outright here and now to be Mrs. Dale Shand and settle down to tranquil domesticity? It's a thought. It's more than a thought. I took the pipe from between my teeth and leaned forward and the phone rang and I didn't ask her.

If old man Leffiney was pleased to hear my voice he was masking it with notable distinction.

'Why the devil haven't you been in touch with me these last two days?' The roar was three thousand miles away, but the way it hit my ear drums it could have been in the same room.

'I'm sorry. I've been to Italy and Switzerland and . . . '

'You've *what*!'

'Look, Mr. Leffiney, this call is costing you money and if we just keep right on yelling at each other the bill is going to be fierce. Will you listen?'

'Shoot,' he said.

I gutted the salient facts down to essentials, enough for him to know what was going on. He said: 'I'm not paying you to rescue young women from hoodlums and murderers. I'm paying you to authenticate an identity and . . . '

'I've already done it, Mr. Leffiney. Benjamin Leffiney, of Old Hall Farm, near Thetford, Norfolk, is your sole living heir.'

'You're positive?'

'I've seen the parish records. I'm going back there now to have photographed copies made for forwarding to you. When do you want Ben Leffiney shipped to New York?'

He didn't answer directly. 'What do you think of him, Shand?' he asked.

'He's a farmer hit by bad luck and possibly by certain personal deficiencies. A man who, after years of being well-known round the district, has tended to withdraw into himself. He seems to be living almost like a recluse, nursing his private woes.'

'H'm . . . '

'Well, I guess it's at least understandable. It's fair to add that he brightened-up considerably when I told him he might be in line for an indecently large fortune. But, then, who wouldn't?'

'Would you?'

'Try me, Mr. Leffiney.'

'You'll collect your fee, your substantiated expenses and the agreed bonus. Pretty easy money for what you've had to do.'

'I'm not complaining. Do you want me to call you from Norfolk? I could put Ben on the line.'

'You can call me, yes — but I'll defer talking to my last relative until he arrives in New York. You'll come with him, of course.'

'Not sure I can guarantee that. I've other work coming up.'

'Mine comes first. Besides, you can be here and back in three days.'

'I can take two, that's about the limit.'

'Very well. Call me tonight at ten o'clock — your time.'

'Right,' I said.

Nancy gave me a cool look. 'Will you be staying overnight in Thetford, Mr. Shand?'

'I guess so. Possibly two.'

'I see,' said Nancy. She sounded faintly distant. I don't know why.

I picked up my Hillman Minx and struggled with some of the world's worst traffic. A Bentley passed me, going the other way. A liveried chauffeur with a get-out-of-my-way expression on his pale face was driving and a man was lolling in the padded rear seats with his eyes closed. He was Juan Francesco . . .

14

I couldn't take his number because the Bentley was immediately swallowed-up in the traffic and a U-turn was not merely illegal but impossible.

It was fully five minutes before I could park near a pay telephone booth and call Logan. Not that the information was going to help him much, though he seemed grateful for it.

'If this blighted Spaniard is in England there could be another art steal on the way,' he said. 'I'll have the specialist boys alerted for a start.'

I got back in my car and drove into Thetford around six in the evening. The lad with the splendid whiskers gave me a genial eye when I walked into his bar.

'Whisky, sir?' he asked, already reaching.

'No, a pint of your excellent bitter.'

'Didn't know you were coming back, sir — thought you'd gone off to London.'

'Some unfinished business here,' I told him.

'Nice to see you again, anyway.' He beamed. 'And you're not the only one who's come back. Miss Travers is here, too.'

'Is she in the hotel right now?'

'Couldn't say, sir. Reception might know . . . oh, she's here now.'

I turned. Linda was framed in the doorway. She stopped, then came forward quickly. 'Why, Dale — you didn't say you were coming down here tonight.'

'I wasn't sure if I'd make it until tomorrow. How are you?'

'I'm fine and it's lovely to be back in England. I don't think I shall ever want to go on holiday in Switzerland or Italy after what happened. I feel so much safer here.'

'Well, you weren't exactly safe in Norfolk, were you?'

'No, that's true — I'd forgotten. But somehow I *feel* safer. I mean the whole atmosphere of England feels safe, despite all the crime and violence one reads in the newspapers. What happened when I went to Grange Manor was out of character here — and the horrible men who kidnapped me weren't English, anyway. Well, they're a long way off now, thank goodness.'

I hesitated for a second. She noticed it and said: 'What's wrong?'

'I saw Francesco in a car on my way out of London,' I said. She had to know.

'Oh . . . '

I steered her to a table and bought her a drink, gin and bitter lemon. 'It doesn't have to mean he's looking for you, Linda. In fact, there's no point now, anyway. The kidnapping was to make sure you couldn't talk. They'll know by now that you *have* talked — to the authorities.'

'Yes . . . ' She said it uncertainly. 'I suppose so, only . . . '

'It's all right, they're not going to get you again. Anyway, you're going to have police protection.'

She made a small laugh. 'Are you going to protect me, too?'

'It's a thought.'

'You're so nice to be with,' she said. 'Have you seen Ben Leffiney again?'

'Not yet. I've only just checked in here.

183

I'm going out to his farm shortly.'

'Can I come with you?'

'No reason why not. We'll eat and then go. I'll phone him to expect us.'

An hour later we were driving through the forest in the gathering dusk. Linda said: 'You haven't told me much about yourself — in a personal way, I mean.'

'We don't seem to have had much time for swapping biographical histories. What do you want to know?'

'All about you. Are you married?'

'No. Why do you ask?'

'Well, for goodness sake, it's something a girl wants to know if she's going out in a car with a man, isn't it?'

'That depends on what the man intends to do or may be thought to be intending.'

'All right, then — what are your intentions towards a young, defenceless girl?'

'I haven't decided what my intentions are.'

'My, how cautious the man is,' she mocked.

'Slow, you mean? I can stop the car and change that.'

'No, keep driving.' She pushed a strand of her hair off her face and went on: 'You haven't always been a private detective, I suppose.'

'No. I used to be a newspaperman on a small-town paper in the Middle West. Then I went to New York.'

'On a newspaper?'

'Yeah, but after a while I became an assistant investigator in the District Attorney's office. But I got out of line several times.'

'How?'

'I have a tendency to act on my own, against the book. It didn't take very well, so I quit and started out as a PI.'

'Do you like it?' she asked curiously.

'Some of it, not all. It's rather a lonesome occupation, though not so solitary as being a writer, which is something else I've thought of becoming.'

'You mean creative writing, like being a novelist or a playwright?'

'Yes. I've had some limited success. I don't know whether I could make a living out of it, but I might try some time.'

'It's difficult, you know — unless you

185

write a book that gets off the ground, as they say in the trade.'

'Why, have you tried?'

'Not since I was at college and then I never finished the book. Very, very few people ever write one that amounts to anything in their teens. Mostly not until they're forty or so.'

'Maybe I'm just getting ready, then.'

'Probably,' she said calmly. 'As for me, I started as a junior reporter on a weekly newspaper, moved to an evening and then a national and finally gravitated to magazines. Perhaps that's what I'm really good at — magazine feature writing. I don't know that I could face the concentrated thinking and the sheer grinding labour of fifty to seventy thousand words.'

I grinned. 'Somebody said that, to a man, professional writers hate writing and loath reading almost as much.'

'Auberon Waugh.'

'Well, *he* writes. I'm inclined to the view that to the professional writing's a kind of love-hate relationship — you may hate the slogging hard work but you hope you'll love the result.'

'Better if the public love it — nothing makes money faster than a really successful book. You'll have to write one.'

I put the Hillman into a left-hand bend and said: 'The trouble is there's no ascertainable formula. In some professions if you get your ingredients in the right proportions you get the right results. In writing it's all chance — even if the book is well written. If there was a formula every novelist could be rich tomorrow. There isn't, though.'

'That's true. Most authors have to take on other work, like journalism — unless they've got enough money to live on while they're struggling for recognition.'

'Well, I had struggles when I first turned private investigator. Things have been rather better in the last few years — more particularly in the last twelve months.'

'You mean you've enough to live on while you write, if you decide to try?'

'I could probably manage four or five years. That ought to be more than enough to find out if I can write a best-seller.'

'Not necessarily. You could produce a string of novels which just earned modest money without ever catching-on in a big way.'

'I love this flattery,' I grinned.

'I'm not making difficulties, Dale, they're ready-made. You could do first-class writing without any of it making a massive impact.'

'Yeah, I know all that. But I still might try some time.'

'Some time — it's no use. I know newspapermen who are always going to write a book some time. Great novelists about to begin, master dramatists who somehow never get started. If you really mean to write you must be willing to do it in the traditional garret, if need be.'

'I guess you're right. Maybe I'm just playing with the idea. Or I'm making too much money. How about you?'

'I told you I'm a journalist. I'm supposed to be good at it. But I don't think I'll ever be even a first-class second-rate novelist. Journalism teaches you a lot, but the episodic nature of the work doesn't condition you for the sustained effort of filling several hundred pages of quarto typescript. No, I haven't got that kind of talent and I know it.'

'You asked if I was married,' I said. 'Are you?'

For a long moment she sat silent. Then she said: 'Yes — or, rather, I was. I divorced him.'

'I'm sorry.'

'That's all right. It was three years ago. He went off with a dolly he met in a discotheque — not the first, but the first I found out about. She was just one in a procession. He couldn't keep his hands off mini skirts.'

'A lot of guys have that impulse.'

'Oh, yes, but mostly it's just a passing fantasy. With Tony it didn't end there. He was older than me, you know. A thirty-five-year-old man who couldn't keep away from the teenage girls.'

'Some fellows are like that.'

'Not you, I hope.'

'I'm on the brink of forty.'

'You're not answering the question. Besides, some of these kids will go to bed with older men at the drop of a hat.'

'I haven't dropped one in that company. I'm not proposing to, if that's an answer.'

'It's all right, I didn't think you were that kind. In fact, I'd say you're a bit old-fashioned.'

I thought of Katie Allison, the girl I had known in England last summer; she had said the same thing, but in the end . . . ah, well. I thought of Linda Travers coming out of a bedroom and kissing me while I slept or while she supposed I was sleeping. All right, what are you going to do about it, Shand? I haven't decided.

She made a small unconscious movement and I could feel the outline of her thigh against mine, briefly. I took a hand off the steering wheel and put it back, not without effort. I guessed she had seen me do it.

Then the turn for Oak Hall Farm showed in the headlights. I drove down it, turned the car in through the open gates and walked with her to the door.

Ben Leffiney opened it. He looked at her in surprise.

'Miss Linda Travers,' I said. 'A friend.

She's also a journalist and will probably want to write you up.'

'Oh, well I don't know that I want any of that,' he said. There was a small edge in the way he said it, then it was gone and he grinned slowly. 'I always put a X in the little box in the football pools coupon, the one about clients not wishing any publicity. If this family business gets plastered all over the newspapers I'll be swamped by bloody begging letters ... I beg your pardon, miss.'

'I don't mind your swearing, Mr. Leffiney. And if you don't want your name published I'll respect your wishes.'

'Well, thanks. You'd better come in.' He held the door open and followed us through to the wide living-room. 'Would you care for a drink?'

I shook my head.

'Thank you, no,' said Linda.

'You won't mind if I have one, will you?' He poured Scotch from the remains of a bottle and said: 'I take it everything's now in order, Mr. Shand?'

'Yes. The parish records establish the

relationship and I've been in touch with Mr. Leffiney in New York, by phone. He wants to see you as soon as you can arrange to fly out.'

'Any time. When do you suggest?' He asked the question with a slight touch of uncertainty.

'Almost immediately. He wants me to accompany you. By the way, you don't have to worry about money — I'm getting the airline tickets and the cost will be on my bill.'

Ben Leffiney put the rest of his drink down, rather noisily. 'Well, that's a relief, I don't mind admitting it. I've had a pretty rough time lately.'

'Yeah, you did tell me that.'

He poured himself another drink. 'I thought you'd be coming to see me a day or so ago.'

'I meant to, but I had to go abroad somewhat suddenly.'

'Abroad?'

'Italy and Switzerland, as a matter of fact.'

He blinked several times, very fast. 'What for?'

'Something happened that made it necessary, Mr. Leffiney.'

'You mean . . . something to do with our business?'

'No, it was another matter.'

He put his glass down. 'I don't understand . . . ' he began. Then he laughed and said: 'If it's not connected with me, what the hell, eh?'

'You could say that.' I lit a cigarette and watched the smoke crawl off the end. The small intermission of silence seemed to make him fidgety. Abruptly, I said: 'It was a police matter.'

He stared. 'But you're not connected with the police . . . I thought you were a private detective.'

'I am, but my business got kind of mixed-up with theirs. Haven't you heard?'

'Heard — heard what?'

'Sir James Arkwright was murdered over at Grange Manor and about a million dollars' worth of art treasures stolen.'

'Good God!' he said. 'Well, I didn't know Arkwright except to nod to. Don't move in his circles. But I certainly didn't know he'd been . . . ' Leffiney let the sentence end, then said: 'I haven't been off the farm in days. I haven't even read the papers or put the radio on. But I don't see where you come into all this.'

'Miss Travers went to the Manor at the time the gang were there. They took her abroad in a private plane. I went after them.'

'Well!' he said. 'So that's where you've been.'

'That's right. I managed to get Miss Travers away from them.'

'Pretty dangerous, wasn't it?'

'At times, Mr. Leffiney.'

He fingered his leather-bound cuffs. 'Who were these chaps?'

'A Spaniard who calls himself Juan Francesco and a couple of other fellows — Borge and Jiri.'

'Oh, yes?' he said politely. 'Well, I'm glad you were able to rescue this young lady.' He looked at her again; he still seemed surprised that she was there. 'You're not from these parts, are you, Miss Travers?'

'No, what makes you ask?'

'Nothing, I just sort of said it.'

'I'm down here working for a magazine . . . '

'Londoner, eh?'

'I was born there. It's funny you asking that, though. I believe my ancestors came from a place not far from here.'

'Oh, where would that be, then?'

'A little place called Diss.'

Ben Leffiney smiled. 'You're almost one of us, after all, Miss Travers. Pretty little spot, Diss, so they tell me . . . ' He stopped and then said: 'I mean everybody likes the place.'

'I mean to visit there before I go back,' Linda said.

He looked down at his hands. They were fine, smooth hands with clear oblong nails. I had a fleeting impression that they were not quite steady, like a hard drinker's hands. He poured another drink, smaller this time, then drove both hands in his pockets and said: 'Well, what's the next move, Mr. Shand?'

I said: 'I've one or two things to see to here and in London. That'll give you time to arrange things on the farm and pack.

I'll book the flights to New York for the day after tomorrow.'

'Fine, I'll be ready. Do you want me to meet you at the airport or are you coming back here?'

'No, you can meet me at Heathrow. I'll telephone you tomorrow.'

'Right, then.'

We went back to the car. Minutes passed with the miles and she hadn't spoken.

I slowed a little and said: 'Anything the matter?'

'Ben Leffiney,' she answered. 'I didn't like him very much.'

'Oh, why?'

'I don't know. I just didn't.'

'You could do worse than make a play for him — he's going to be stinking rich.'

'Ugh!' she said. 'I don't like money that much. I'd rather have . . . ' She let the rest of it go unspoken.

I didn't take her up on it. I drove back to Thetford and Power seemed pleased to see me. 'Had Logan on the phone. I gather you saw this feller Francesco in London. That makes it a Yard matter as well as one for us. D'you think Borge is with him?'

'I don't know. It's a possibility.'

'Well, there's nothing more I can do here,' Power said. 'I'm going back to Norwich tonight. We'll be in touch with the Metropolitan boys and whatever they turn up. Are you staying on here, Miss Travers?'

'Another day, perhaps two days.'

Power smiled. 'We'll be looking after you this time. I don't suppose these fellows will come back here, though, despite the old saying about murderers returning to the scene of their crime.'

She shivered.

'We've got your signed statement and we shan't be needing you again until there's an arrest — if we make one,' went on Power philosophically.

I said slowly: 'Francesco is the brains behind the art stealing and if he's back in England that suggests another coup is being put in train.'

'So Logan feels.' Power grinned faintly. 'Putting a guard on every private collection in every shire in England's a tall order.'

'It might be a raid on a public collection — a major gallery or something like that.'

'Possible. Well, we'll have to see. They're trying to find his whereabouts now — but it's my bet this Spanish feller has a new English name and an address we know nothing about. Bit like looking for a needle in a haystack. We'll all be trying, though. That way something usually turns up . . . though not always.' He offered his strong, sinewy hand. 'Hope to see you again before this little lot is over, Mr. Shand.'

'I'll count the moments, inspector,' I said with a grin.

'Yes, do,' he said affably and went out.

We got back to the hotel and sat in the bar. It was 9.30 p.m. An hour later, Linda said: 'I think I'll go on up, Dale.'

'I could use some sleep myself,' I said. I knocked my pipe out and we went up the stairs together. Her room was in the same corridor. She put the tabbed key in the lock and suddenly held her face up to be kissed.

'You're nice,' she said simply. 'Did you know I kissed you while you were on Alberto's settee?'

'Yes.' My voice sounded thick.

'I thought you did. You could have . . . '

'What?'

'Nothing.'

She went through the doorway, not saying goodnight. I came in and closed the door. She said unsteadily: 'I'm not . . . not like that to . . . '

'I'm sorry. I'll go.'

She turned then. 'I meant I'm not like that to anybody . . . you do give up easily, don't you?'

I took her in my arms and held her clinging to me. I hadn't any words left.

But for a long time we didn't need any . . .

15

I drove back to London alone and was in my office only minutes after Nancy opened it. She gave me her bright open smile. I met it with an irrational feeling of guilt. I hoped it wasn't showing.

'Everything settled, Mr. Shand?' she asked.

'Yeah — I mean yes. I have to fly to New York with Ben Leffiney tomorrow. Will you book the flight — one single, one return.'

'The return is for you.'

'That's right. I'll be back inside three days, probably less. Anything happening?'

'Mr. Kenning would like you to attend a conference at the weekend. That should fit in nicely. You'll be back by then.'

'I don't know that I can manage it . . . ' I began.

Nancy gave me a mute look of interrogation.

'I mean I may have a social engagement.'

'I see.'

'Dammit, I'm entitled to some social life.'

'But, of course, Mr. Shand.' She reached for the phone. 'Shall I get Mr. Kenning on the wire and cancel?'

'No, tell him I'll be there — wherever it is.'

'The Old Gables at Goring-on-Thames — Mr. Kenning's home. Twelve noon Sunday. I got the impression it's a big assignment Mr. Kenning wants you to handle.'

I nodded. The phone rang. It was Logan. 'No luck trying to locate your Spanish chum,' he said. 'It was a lot to hope for, anyway ... probably got a completely new identity and we've never even set eyes on the chap. There *is* something, though.'

'Oh, what's that?'

'Ever heard of Lester Glanville?'

'It has a kind of faint ring, but, no, I can't place it. Should I?'

'I thought perhaps you might. He's an American, comes from Dallas, Texas. Not quite so rich as that character with the income of £75,000 a day, but rich enough to be going on with.'

'Sounds like a fellow I ought to get to know.'

'Well, you might. Glanville is an international art collector and he's just taken up residence down in Cornwall — a whacking great place near St. Mawes.'

'And?'

Logan made his small dry chuckle. 'If this gang are back in England they might be planning another big steal. Just that.'

'*And* again?'

'I thought you might possibly be interested.'

'I'm interested, but not involved, not this time. I have something else to do.'

'Oh, what?'

'I'm flying to New York tomorrow with this fellow Leffiney.'

Logan said: 'I'd like you to postpone that trip, Shand.'

'I've made all the arrangements.'

'You'd better unmake them, then.'

'Why, for Pete's sake?'

'If an attempt is made on Glanville's collection — which is one of the most valuable in the world — you'll be needed.'

'I don't see that.'

'You've had direct personal contact with Francesco and those associated with him. You're an important witness — what you chaps in the States call a material witness.'

'Look,' I said, 'I *have* to be in New York. But I'll be back inside three days. Will that do?'

'If you guarantee to return in that time, all right.'

'You have my word. I have no intention of staying on in New York — nearly all my work is here now, anyway. But aren't you jumping the gun somewhat?'

'Meaning this gang may not be planning anything in Cornwall?'

'Well, you've no proof that they are, have you?'

'None whatever,' said Logan amiably. 'But we regard it as a possibility, perhaps more than that. You play hunches now and again, I believe.'

'Sometimes, yeah.'

'We're playing one now,' he said quietly.

'What are you proposing to do, immediately?'

'The police down there are putting a guard on Glanville's place — Harbold House it's called. It's just outside St. Mawes, near the old church of St. Just in Roseland.'

'The name sounds poetic, I like it.'

'Yes, it fits the scenery. The church overlooks an inlet from the sea, like a placid lake. Beautiful spot. We're sending some of our own chaps down this afternoon.'

'Wish you luck, Logan.'

'We'll need to catch the bastards red-handed. Of course, nothing may happen — we may be barking up a wrong tree. But we have to try. For one thing, this mob will know about Glanville. That makes him an obvious target.'

'I guess it does. I like the idea of Francesco and his chums facing a long stretch in Dartmoor — though Borge at least ought to go to the scaffold.'

'We don't execute them now, Shand.'

'So I understand.'

'A life sentence which, with remission,

means the bastards are out in less than ten years. Crazy, isn't it?'

'I don't know that it's for me to offer strictures on British procedures,' I said.

'You're too kind to us. See you in three days, then — perhaps we'll have something to tell you then, eh?'

'I hope you do, superintendent.'

I ate, went back to Baker Street and Nancy said: 'I'd better get Ben Leffiney on the line for you, he'll need to know the flight time.'

She called the 100 operator. After a few moments she put the receiver down and said: 'It's ringing out, but he's not answering.'

'That's odd. He told me he hadn't left the farm in days.'

'Well, he must go out and see to the cows and pigs and things, surely?'

'I suppose so. Try again later, Nancy.'

I sat around the office poisoning myself with cigarettes. I had a curious sensation of uneasiness. No reason, I just had it. The phone rang. It was Linda.

'I finished what I was doing earlier than I expected and I'm back in town,' she announced. 'Are you coming round to see me?'

'I don't even know where you live.'

She laughed. 'So you don't. It's Flat 11b Merton Crescent, just off Russell Square. I'll be in tonight. Alone.'

'Not for long you won't.'

'That's good, I . . . never mind, I don't want your head to get too big for your hat.'

'The one I dropped, you mean?'

'Six-thirty would be a nice time,' she said.

I hung up. Nancy asked: 'What was that?' I noticed she avoided saying who.

'Just somebody I know.'

'Oh, a social call. I'm sorry.' She fussed with some papers on her desk and called the farm four more times in the next fifty minutes. No reply.

I made up my mind. 'I'm going back to Ben Leffiney's place,' I said.

Her eyes widened. 'Why — do you think something's wrong?'

'Not necessarily, but I must get through to him. He may be out in the fields or in the town. If I'm there I'll find him. I'll be back tonight.'

It was early afternoon when I got there. He didn't answer the door. Nobody did. I looked around outside. If the hired man was at work I didn't see him. I didn't see anyone. The curious feeling of uneasiness I had had in my office came back, stronger. I went down the back of the farmhouse, along a narrow strip of badly-arranged crazy paving. Although the day was warm all the windows were closed. I reached the end of the crazy paving and turned down the other side. A small window was half open.

I didn't even stop to think. I got it wide open and thrust a leg over the sill. I was in a small room, a small dusty room littered with agricultural junk. The door led into the rear part of the passage which cut through the double-fronted house. I went from room to room, upstairs and downstairs, including the bathroom and lavatory.

Ben Leffiney wasn't anywhere. I walked back into the living-room as the phone rang. I hesitated, then picked up the receiver.

'Oak Hall Farm?' The voice on the line made it a question, but didn't wait for an answer. 'Listen, there's something moving, you're wanted tonight and . . . are you there?'

I said yes in a voice that wasn't mine, but it wasn't Ben Leffiney's, either. There was an abrupt click and the line went dead.

For a long moment I stood there with the receiver still jammed against my left ear. Thoughts whirled in my head, making no sense.

There didn't seem to be any sense in Helmut Borge calling Ben Leffiney on the telephone.

16

Slowly, I put the receiver down on its rest. I let it stay there a second, then picked it up again and dialled the exchange.

'I've just taken a call — can you trace it for me?'

'When was this, sir?'

'Less than a minute ago.'

'Hold on — I'll find out for you.'

I lit a cigarette and dragged on the smoke. The wait seemed interminable, though it wasn't. Then the operator was back. 'The call was made from a public telephone kiosk at St. Mawes, Cornwall, sir.'

'Thanks,' I said thickly.

'I can give you the number, if you wish.'

'No, it doesn't matter,' I said. 'But you can get me one.'

'What number do you wish to call, sir?'

I told her and got through to New Scotland Yard. Logan was in; he always seemed to be in. I could almost see his eyebrows lifting.

'You're quite sure it was Borge ringing the farm?' he asked levelly.

'I'm sure.'

'Then your farming friend must be up to the neck in the art stealing.'

'That's how it looks, yeah.'

'Yet he's going to inherit a vast fortune.'

'He didn't know that until a day or two ago when I told him.'

'As recently as that?'

'Yes, but there's something else.'

'Oh? You mean connected with the art stealing and the Arkwright murder?'

'I don't know about that. But ever since I met him I've had a feeling there's something about Ben Leffiney — something not quite on the level.'

'One of *your* hunches?'

'Perhaps, I'm not sure. Frankly, I don't know what it is, but it's something.'

'If he *is* one of this mob that'd be it.'

'Could be.'

'Well, thanks for ringing me, anyway. Incidentally, if they try anything down in

Cornwall they'll think they've stirred up a nest of hornets.'

'Why, is the place surrounded with cops?'

'Not exactly surrounded. A regional crime squad car is standing by, in the lane near the house. Nothing can get in or out without being spotted.'

'Sounds good enough.'

'It should be. Also, we're being discreet. Don't want to ring the whole damned place with uniformed branch chaps and scare the enemy off before they've even started. If a raid's being planned we'll let it take place — then catch them in the act.'

'These fellows are dangerous,' I said.

'We can be pretty dangerous, too, if we have to,' Logan rejoined. 'Are you staying on down there?'

'Well, I'd better try to locate Ben Leffiney — he's supposed to be flying with me to New York tomorrow.'

Logan said distinctly: 'I think you'd better cancel that flight, Shand. If Leffiney is in any way connected with the art stealing we shall require him for questioning.'

'I only said he's *supposed* to be flying with me, Logan. If there's a link between him and Francesco he obviously isn't going to be allowed out of the country. What I can't figure is why he isn't here.'

'Well, if you find him ring us immediately . . . and don't let him get away.'

'What do you expect me to do — arrest him?'

'If necessary, yes,' said Logan coolly.

I hung up and stood in the middle of the room trying to think. Maybe Ben Leffiney had got himself into a financial jam and had taken money for acting as finger man for the heist mob? It was feasible. But where *was* he? A new thought stirred — it was also feasible that, knowing he was going to be rich, he simply wanted out and they had sent somebody to kill him and Borge had called the farm to make sure and realized he wasn't talking to the killer. No — that didn't stand up. Borge had spoken as if he were talking to Ben.

I tried again, going back over the last conversation I had had with him. There

212

had been something vaguely off-key about his manner, even about the way he had talked to Linda; not least when she had said that her ancestors came from a place called Diss. Or was I imagining that? I didn't know.

But Helmut Borge had called Ben Leffiney on the phone and that had to carry significance. Yet I was oppressed by the feeling that there was something else — something totally different, not necessarily fusing with the art robbery and the murder or anything else that had happened since I got into this business. You're still imagining things, Shand . . .

I stared round the room. Everything looked the way it had been when I was here before. I sniffed at the air. No reek of cordite, not even the merest whisper of it. Maybe Leffiney had just gone into town or up to London or anywhere — even Cornwall. No, he wouldn't do it. Why the hell should he? Ben Leffiney was waiting for me to phone him, waiting to fly three thousand miles to call on twenty-two million dollars. But he *wasn't* waiting, was he?

Mechanically, I went round the room opening and closing desk drawers, sliding back the glass panel of the bookcase. A book fell out. I picked it up to return it and a piece of notepaper slid from between the pages. On it was written, in hardpoint pencil, a series of entries in column form. At the top were the words *Town, Assay, Date and Duty Marks.* And below, in separate columns referring to London, were tabulated entries. These included dates from the middle of the last century and references to Leopard's Head, Lion Passant and Queen's Head.

The entries continued down the page and were followed by the start of another, covering Newcastle upon Tyne and beginning 1839–40. Another series showed York and the city's sign. After that came a pencilled note — *ref. English Goldsmiths and Their Marks, C. J. Jackson.* Then the entries finished as if they hadn't been completed.

But their meaning was clear if you had knowledge and I had just enough. All articles made of silver or silver-gilt carry these kind of marks and during the last century they included the mark of the office where the piece was assayed, the alphabetical date letter, the maker's mark and the assay and duty marks. From 1784 to 1890 a tax was levied on all silver assayed in Britain and to show it had been paid the piece was stamped with the sovereign's head.

The notes had the appearance of being put down for reference. If they meant anything, in the context of what had lately been going on, it was that Ben Leffiney was interested in Victorian plate — and it was now too much of a coincidence to suppose that the interest was wholly innocent.

Yet I still had the feeling that there was something else . . . but what?

I went across the room, stumbling on a loose floorboard, and out into the farmyard. The whole place was deserted except for cows grazing in the big meadow behind the range of barns. The silence and the sense of desertion seemed inexplicable. I got into my car and drove down the narrow lane to the forest road, cruising up to the *Give Way* sign and waiting for another car to pass. A face in the car smiled a greeting, the face of Canon Varley. He went a little way down the road, stopped and waved a hand. I came out of the T-junction and braked behind him and got out.

'I was thinking of calling on Ben,' he said. 'How is he?'

'I've just been there, canon — he seems to be out.'

'Oh? You sound as if that surprised you.'

'A little, yes. He was expecting me.'

'Some business about the fortune he's to inherit, eh?'

'As a matter of fact, yes. I've made arrangements for him to fly to New York in the morning. Well, I guess I'll just have to call back later.'

The reverend looked at me and said: 'You could try the local hospital.'

'How's that?'

'He's been having out-patient treatment there, you know.'

'I didn't, canon. What was the trouble?'

'He cut his hand while using a scythe. Mind you, that was a few weeks ago and he may have ceased going for dressings.'

'Which hand was it?'

'The left, I believe — why?'

'Nothing,' I said. But there was. I heard myself saying: 'Would the cut still show?'

'I imagine so, it had to be stitched — I recall his telling me. That was — ah — before he took the notion of staying away from church and, I believe, pretty well everything else.'

'Well, thanks, rector. I'll certainly call at the hospital.'

He told me how to get there and drove on down the road. I turned the car round and went back towards Thetford. Less than twenty minutes later I knew that Ben Leffiney hadn't been there.

The casualty ward sister said: 'He was supposed to come in for a final check, but he didn't.' She smiled faintly. 'That's not entirely unusual — the patient feels better and just doesn't bother.'

'What sort of a cut was it?'

'Deep, but not serious. We put seven stitches in.' She eyed me for a moment, then went on: 'I take it you're a friend?'

'Yes. He didn't keep an appointment

and Canon Varley, whom I met by chance, suggested he might be here.'

'Oh, I see. Well, I'm afraid we haven't seen him for some time. Mind you, I expect his cut is healing up quite nicely.'

'There'll be a scar, I imagine.'

'Oh, yes. It'll go fainter, but not for some time.'

I went out with my head full of thoughts, but now only one mattered: the thought that Ben Leffiney's hands were smooth and firm and unscarred . . .

I parked at the back of the hotel. The girl behind the reception desk gave me a wide eye and said: 'Back *again*, Mr. Shand?'

'Only briefly this time. I'd like to use the phone.'

She smiled assent and I called Linda's flat because if I was going to have to stay on here for hours we wouldn't be able to meet tonight. I could hear the ringing tone, but that was all I heard. Not Shand's lucky day. I put the receiver down, picked it up again and tried to get Ben Leffiney. No good.

The girl at the reception said: 'You seem to be having a lot of trouble.'

'Yes. I can't even get through to Oak Hall Farm. I thought these fellows never left the farm except to go to cattle sales.'

'Oh, they get about, you know.' She put a glass paperweight on a small stack of accounts and went on: 'Mr. Leffiney seems to be in demand today. We had a gentleman in not ten minutes ago asking the way to the farm.'

I stared: 'You mean a stranger?'

'Well, he must have been, mustn't he?'

I nodded absently. There wasn't any reason why someone shouldn't ask the way to Oak Hall Farm, but I had an odd feeling about it just the same. Anything having to do with Ben Leffiney was odd right now. I became aware that the receptionist was looking at me curiously and said: 'Can you describe this man?'

'I think so. Why, do you . . . '

'I might know him,' I lied.

'Well, he was fortyish, about medium height and a bit on the thick-set side. Rather ordinary-looking, if you know what I mean.'

The description meant nothing. I shrugged and was about to leave when she said: 'I thought it was funny him asking the way.'

'Why was that?'

'His voice — I mean he sounded as if he came from round here. Of course, he could have come originally from some other part of Norfolk . . . '

'How do you mean — originally?'

'I thought he must've been abroad, in America. He had a car outside, an old Austin. I noticed a suitcase on the back seats with Pan-Am labels stuck on it.' She smiled again. 'I wasn't being nosey — I could see it through the window.'

I didn't answer. Suddenly, I was remembering the non-existent name at the non-existent address in Philadelphia: Peter Adelberger, the man who had written to old Jesse Melford Leffiney and started the whole thing going.

Finally, I said: 'Did he give his name?'

'No, he just walked in and asked the way.' The curiosity in her face and her voice was undisguised now.

I said thanks and got back in my car.

Fifteen minutes later I was back at the farm and an old dark green Austin Cambridge was parked outside it. I looked in the car and went up the farmyard and found him standing by the door. He heard me and started turning. 'Is that you . . . ' Then he saw me and added: 'Sorry, I thought you must be Ben Leffiney.'

'He's out.'

'Oh — why, have you been here before?'

'Quite recently. Like you, I'm trying to find him.'

He eyed me uncertainly. 'Are you a friend of Ben's, then?'

'I'm not sure you could call me a friend — more a bearer of good news.'

His eyes, which were a very pale blue, flickered. 'I don't quite follow that . . . ' he began.

'He's the heir to a very large fortune, Mr. Adelberger.'

That stirred him up all right. He almost jumped off the doorstep. 'I . . . I beg your pardon,' he said.

'Granted.'

'My name happens to be Philip Loomis, not what you said.'

'So I noticed from the labels on your suitcase. But the stickers say Philadelphia to London via New York. A fellow calling himself Peter Adelberger wrote to Jesse Melford Leffiney from that city. Check?'

'I don't know what you're talking about, Mr . . . ?'

'Shand is the name. I'm acting for old Mr. Leffiney in New York.'

He turned a heavy gold signet ring on the third finger of his left hand, which enabled him not to look directly at me, and said: 'What has all this to do with me?'

'That's what I'm beginning to wonder, Mr. Adelberger.'

'Loomis. I told you my name.'

'You did and I don't doubt it because there's no such person as Peter Adelberger and no such address as the one he gave in Philadelphia. Why did you do that?'

'Do what?'

'Don't be coy, Mr. Loomis. The coincidence is too strong. You wrote to old Mr. Leffiney about encountering his very unusual name and for some reason you chose to call yourself Adelberger.'

'I'm not listening to any more of this nonsense,' he said with a fine show of rage. 'I'm going.'

'Without seeing Ben?'

'He's not in. I . . . I'll call back later.'

I planted himself right in front of him. He looked up uneasily. 'Let me pass, please.'

'Ben Leffiney is missing,' I said. 'Suppose I report it to the local police and take you along for questioning?'

'What the hell are you talking about?'

'There's been one murder round here in the last few days, Mr. Loomis. How do I know there hasn't been another?'

'For God's sake, you don't think I've killed Ben?' he yelled.

'Frankly, no. You wouldn't be knocking on his door if you had. But he's disappeared and I could make things disagreeable for you with the local cops, for a time at least. They take you in and put out a statement about a man helping them with their inquiries.'

He tongued his lips, then seemed to recover some self-possession. 'You're talking a load of old codswallop,' he sneered. 'I'm a friend of Ben's. I've just got back from a business trip to the States and decided to look him up.'

'Yet you had to ask the way here.'

'How the hell do *you* know?'

'The receptionist at the Feathers Hotel mentioned it.'

'So what? I've been here before, but it was only once, in the dark, and I wasn't driving. I wasn't quite sure of the route.'

'Understandable — and it doesn't matter, anyway. What *does* matter is why you called yourself Peter Adelberger when you wrote to old Mr. Leffiney.'

'I still don't know what the bloody hell you're talking about.'

'I think you do. In fact, I'm starting to have a lot of peculiar thoughts about both you and Ben Leffiney.'

'I'm not standing here listening to any more of this crap,' he stormed.

'Let's go in and wait, then.'

'What!'

'There's a window open round the back.'

His jaw sagged. 'You . . . you've been in before?'

'Sure. Once with Ben and once looking for him.' I took hold of Loomis's arm and propelled him round the back of the farmhouse. He was frightened now and showed it. Well, I was a good four inches taller.

We went into the living-room and sat staring at each other from faded leather armchairs like a couple of long-lost brothers who had never cared for one another in the first place.

'Look, this is crazy . . . ' he muttered.

'Everything about this business is crazy, Mr. Loomis. In particular, it's crazy that you go all the way to America to write a letter under a phoney name to a man you've never met.'

'I keep telling you I know nothing about that . . . '

'That's right, you keep telling me. But I keep on not believing you, Mr. Loomis. Maybe I'm crazy, but I don't think so.' I jumped the automatic into my hand and pointed it at him. 'You've got five seconds to start talking it up, my friend.'

He sat there, his face like cold wet suet. Then his hands started to shake. He clenched the fingers together hard, but it didn't stop the shaking.

I crossed one thigh over the other and held the gun along the uppermost one, still aiming. 'I'll help you to get started, Mr. Loomis. There's something odd about Ben Leffiney, something I sensed almost from the first time we met. Perhaps even before that, when I found out that nobody named Adelberger lived at a Philadelphia address which doesn't exist. I thought maybe it could be some kind of mix-up. Then I found out something else — that Ben Leffiney, apparently a sociable fellow, had virtually become a recluse. At first that could be explained because of pressing money worries, which are apparently real enough. But something emerged today which can't be explained. Ben Leffiney got a deep cut on his left hand while at work, a cut which needed seven stitches . . . and there isn't any trace of it on his hand.'

'Christ!' whispered Loomis. 'He . . . '

'He forgot about it or he didn't notice it,' I said.

Sweat was pooling down Loomis's ashen face. He wasn't shaking again; now he was sitting there petrified. His tongue moved across his lips again and he said: 'You . . . you *know*?'

'I think I do, Mr. Loomis. Everything figures, doesn't it? *The guy I met here isn't Ben Leffiney!*'

Loomis made a small dry sound far back in his throat. He struggled for words. They came out in a jumble of incoherencies. 'It . . . it wasn't my idea . . . I didn't . . . I mean he got me to . . . '

'He found out that a rich old man in New York had the unusual name of Leffiney and got you to contact him because you were going to the States on some business, is that it?'

Loomis nodded dumbly. Then: 'He thought it was a . . . a better way of doing it, better than him making the move, he said.'

'*Who is he?*'

'Joe Holburn, he comes from Norwich,' Loomis said huskily.

'Go on.'

'He ran a small business and used to import stuff from America. Not much, just a bit. It was a firm of which old Leffiney was a director and his name was on the notepaper.' Loomis tried not to look at the gun and went on: 'Joe happened to be in Thetford and heard of Ben Leffiney and he got this idea . . . '

'You mean he found out that old Leffiney was rich and got the idea of latching-on to a vast fortune which, if the relationship was substantiated, rightly belonged to another man. So he gets you to tip old Leffiney off just to make the whole thing look innocent, even accidental.'

He nodded again, not speaking. His eyes swivelled to the automatic, darted away. Then he said: 'I had some inquiry correspondence with this firm, using the name Adelberger. Just as a cover. Then I wrote to Mr. Leffiney.'

'You knew he'd react, Loomis. More than that, by this time you both knew the direct relationship was a fact. All that mattered was whether old Leffiney would bite — and he did.'

'Yes.' He swallowed hardly.

'So Holburn set himself up as Ben Leffiney — resigned from the church, quit going around, staying literally holed-up on the farm so that no one would see him. How much like Ben is he to look at?'

'When he'd shaved off his moustache and beard there was a fair resemblance, but anybody who knew would spot the difference. That's why he kept to the farm.'

I looked at him and said harshly: 'There's one more thing, just one thing you haven't explained — *what happened to the real Ben Leffiney?*'

'He . . . he's been taken care of . . . '

'I hope you don't mean you've murdered him,' I said.

'For God's sake, no . . . '

'*What happened?*'

Loomis ran a finger round the inside of his collar. 'We . . . all right, we decided to hold him prisoner here while Joe took his place and claimed the inheritance, if old Leffiney showed real interest. If he didn't we were just going to pack it in.'

'Don't play games with me,' I snarled. 'If old man Leffiney started inquiries Holburn was going to present himself as the sole heir — and that left you both with the problem of what to do with Ben.'

'We . . . we hadn't decided . . . I mean . . . '

'You'd have to kill him, wouldn't you?'

For the first time since he had sat looking at the gun Loomis showed a touch of spirit. 'You've no right to make me incriminate myself, no right even to question me!'

'I've more right than you think, Loomis. I'm asking, for the last time, what have you done with Ben Leffiney?'

'All right then. We've done nothing to him — nothing. He's here — here on this farm.'

I remembered the loose floorboard I had stumbled over. But they wouldn't need to pull the floor up. I said tightly: 'Show me.'

He got out of the chair and shambled across the room. Nobody ever looked more defeated, but I put the barrel of the gun in his back just the same. Shand taking no chances.

We went along the passage and out into the yard and he pointed down a slope. There was a door at the bottom and some heavy sections of wood. It simply hadn't occurred to me to look in the cellar.

'You first, Mr. Loomis,' I said.

He teetered down the slope, stopped and said: 'I forgot — Joe has the key.'

I put the gun against the lock and triggered it. There was a hard snapping sound as the lock fractured. I shouldered the door wide open. Light flooded in behind us. A tousled man with his shirt wide open at the neck blinked and started to crawl off a pile of sacking. Then he saw the gun and sank back.

'It's all right, Mr. Leffiney,' I said. 'You're with friends — with one, anyway.'

He was unshaven and dirty and looked more than half-way to being ill. His mouth opened but no words came. He stared past me at Loomis and put out a trembling finger.

'You're with him . . . you must be one of the bloody swine who . . . '

'I told you I'm a friend,' I said. 'You're free. Do you understand? You're free.'

Slowly, as if movement was a physical pain, he stood up. There was a sudden small sound behind me and there shouldn't have been any sound because I ought not to have shown Loomis my back. The sound was made by the door swinging shut. Something heavy was hurriedly wedged against it, then a mad scramble of footsteps.

Loomis was making his getaway.

17

It took me perhaps a minute and a half to get the door open, after which it was no use looking for Loomis. His car had gone. I didn't even care much.

I turned back to Ben Leffiney. He was standing with his shoulders against the dank wall of the cellar. He began shivering.

'You're ill,' I said.

He nodded. 'I feel lousy, I've been down here weeks, I think. I don't know for sure, I lost count. Every day seemed endless. The last few days I've been terribly cold, although it's summer. I think I've got the 'flu.'

'I'll get you out of here,' I said. I put an arm round his shoulders and steered him up the slope and into the farmhouse. I could feel him shivering and once I had to prop him up so that he didn't fall. Then we were in the living-room. I made him whisky and hot water with lemon juice squeezed into it. I asked if he had any aspirin.

'In the kitchen — second drawer in the dresser.'

I went back to the kitchen and found the bottle. It was about a quarter full. The aspirin was soluble and I put four in a small glass of water.

'You'd better soak yourself in a hot bath and get into bed,' I said.

'I'll be all right . . . '

'Famous last words,' I said. 'I'm going to call your doctor.'

He stirred the aspirin, drank it in one and said again: 'I'll be all right.'

'Who is he?'

'Are all you Yanks so persistent?' he said with a faint grin.

'I couldn't say, but this one is. What was the name you were about to tell me?'

'I wasn't.'

'Give, Ben!'

'All right. Dr. Jamison.'

I got the number from him and called the surgery. A woman's voice said Dr. Jamison was expected back within about ten minutes and that the message would be passed to him. I lit a cigarette and asked Ben Leffiney if he felt equal to talking.

'Yes, I can talk.' The hot toddy seemed to be going to work on him. I fixed another.

'You'd better have one yourself,' he said.

While I was getting it he said wonderingly: 'I don't even know how to begin thanking you. For God's sake, I don't even know who you are!'

'Dale Shand — I'm a private investigator formerly based in New York City but as of now operating from London.'

'Look,' he said, 'how do you come to . . . to be mixed up in all this?'

I told him — the lot. He sat there nursing his second whisky and not even sipping it. At the finish I said: 'I was here a short while ago looking for Ben Leffiney — or the guy who took your identity. Didn't you hear me?'

'I heard something, yes. I didn't call out because I thought it was him . . . this bugger Holburn.'

'He'd threatened you?'

'He said he'd kill me if I so much as opened my mouth.'

'They were going to kill you in the end, Ben — if the deal went through. Most likely tonight — before Holburn flew to America with me.'

He drank three parts of the hot Scotch. 'I realized what they'd do, Mr. Shand, but . . . ' A smile moved on his ravaged face. 'I just thought while there's life there's hope. Not much, but there wouldn't have been any if I'd started making a rumpus to attract attention.'

'No, I can see that all right.'

'Not that it'd have done much good, anyway. This farm is right on its own.'

'So I noticed. How about the hired help, though?'

'I only had one man — Jed Harker it was. Holburn sent Loomis with a message saying he wasn't needed any more. That must've been a week or two ago.'

'I see. Did they tell you what the whole thing was about?'

'Some of it, not in detail.' Leffiney finished off his drink and went on slowly:

'*Is* it right about me inheriting this fortune?'

'You're the man all right, Ben. Mind you, the fortune doesn't flow your way until the old man dies. But you're his sole heir.'

He bent both knuckles and rubbed them against his eyelids. He took the knuckles away and said: 'It . . . it seems fantastic. I can't believe it . . . '

'You'll get used to the idea after a while,' I said with a grin.

'I never even knew there were any Leffineys in America until Holburn taunted me with coming into the money in my name,' Ben Leffiney said. He stared down at his hands, looked up suddenly and added: 'Suppose Holburn comes back?'

'He'll wish he hadn't, Ben.'

'It's funny him going off. I don't understand it, unless he's up to something else. With these art stealers, I mean. Are you sure he's in with them?'

'I'm sure.'

'Well, I suppose so, but . . . '

'He has to be. The phone call to this

farm from Borge proves that much.'

'But why would he be mixed-up with these bastards if he was going to get old Leffiney's money?'

'Like I said, the heir doesn't jump straight into the money. So he wouldn't get it immediately, though I dare say the old man would be generous. Besides, Holburn must have been tied-in with this gang before he knew about Leffiney or you.'

'I suppose so.'

'It's clear enough,' I said. 'The Leffiney heir business came later, a kind of bonus. I'd say it has nothing whatever to do with the art steal.'

'What about Loomis?'

'He was in the Leffiney affair with Holburn — between them they cooked-up the idea of Loomis making the initial approach, so that the thing would appear to arise just by a happy chance. That's how it all stood until I got into it.'

Ben Leffiney looked directly at me. 'I still don't know how to thank you . . . ' he began.

'Don't bother, Ben. All that matters is that the right guy will be making his claim after all. There's one hell of a shock coming for Holburn.'

Ben fingered his stubbly chin. 'I still don't understand where he's got to,' he said.

'Borge said something about a job, kind of reminding him.' A thought came to me and I went on: 'Have any of your farm vehicles — a truck, say — been used while they kept you in that cellar?'

'Why, yes, now you mention it. One of the two lorries went out a few nights ago, but not for long. Then . . . '

He paused and I said: 'The Arkwright treasures were stashed away on a small plane, or a lot of them — but anything really bulky would have to go by road — in a truck and preferably one they hadn't either bought or stolen.'

Ben stared.

'Yours would do swell,' I said tersely.

He went on staring and I resumed: 'The gang are thought to be setting up a new raid — on a place down in Cornwall. It's my guess they ordered Holburn to drive your truck down there.'

Ben Leffiney leaned forward. 'I was going to tell you — the lorry went out earlier today and hasn't come back. I thought at first that Loomis might've taken it, but that's impossible, as he's just been here.'

'You're sure about this, Ben?'

He nodded. 'It went out all right and it hasn't come back. Leastways, I haven't heard it.'

'And you would have?'

'Most of the time I would — but I've felt so ill I dozed off periodically. But you can find out. I've two lorries and they're kept in one of the outbuildings — the far one, near the smaller of the two gates which lead on to the field.'

I went out and looked. When I came back I said: 'One of them isn't there.'

'You're right, then — Holburn must be on his way to Cornwall.'

I said slowly: 'Borge called this place to remind Holburn of some job — but Holburn wasn't here to take the call. I took it — and Borge knew almost at once that he wasn't talking with Holburn.'

'Then what . . . ' Ben Leffiney let the words trail away from him.

I thought back to Borge calling the farm. That clearly meant Holburn was involved with them; almost certainly had been before he even knew of the Leffiney lode and got the idea of hijacking another man's inheritance. Everything figured — except for one factor. Holburn was expecting me to come through on the phone with the flight time and he would *have* to know that. Yet he wasn't at the farm and hadn't been there in hours. Maybe if I stuck around he would show and . . .

Even as the unspoken words formed themselves in my mind I jumped at the answer; perhaps jump wasn't really the right word because I ought to have guessed it before.

I went fast across the room. Ben Leffiney said: 'Now what?'

But I didn't answer. I grabbed the telephone and called my office. Nancy's voice came over, cool and composed as usual. You'd need to come through with the news that the end of the world was starting and Judgment Day setting in with unusual severity to get a change in the tone of Nancy's agreeable voice.

'Yes, Mr. Shand?'

'Nancy,' I said, 'have you had a phone call from Ben Leffiney?'

'Yes, it was about two hours ago. He said he'd had to leave the farm on a matter of business.'

'Oh, he did, did he?'

'You sound somewhat irritated.'

'You haven't got the right word, but never mind — go on.'

'Well, he was naturally somewhat worried, because he had meant to be at the farm to take a call from you. But it's all right,' added Nancy brightly. 'I was able to tell him the time of the flight and to meet you at Heathrow.'

'That's great . . . '

'You sound in a somewhat odd humour,' said Nancy. 'Is something wrong?'

'Yeah, plenty.'

'I thought there must be . . . ' She paused, clearly waiting for me to tell her, so I did.

'Well, for heaven's sake,' cried Nancy. 'You *are* having a swell time.'

'I guess you could call it that. Did he say where he was calling from?'

'No, he just asked about the flight arrangements, said thanks and rang off. But he wasn't speaking from Thetford.'

'Oh, how do you know that?'

'Thetford's not on the STD system and I heard the rapid pips.'

I let a chuckle drift down the line. 'You ought to be in the private investigation business yourself, Nancy . . . '

'I already am,' said Nancy calmly.

'So you are, I was forgetting.'

'I've been in it or partly in it for a long time, one way and another, but since you opened in London it's been official. Never mind that, though. The thing is he wasn't calling from Thetford.'

'Interesting. Still it doesn't mean he was making the call round the corner from the office, either.'

'No. In fact, we've no way of knowing where he was calling from, have we?'

'Damn!'

'It doesn't matter, really,' murmured

Nancy. 'After all, you'll be seeing him at Heathrow in the morning.'

I laughed. 'Yeah — I want to see his face when the real Ben Leffiney walks in with me.'

'Is there a strong resemblance between them?' asked Nancy curiously.

'A general resemblance, but it would only pass if Holburn more or less kept out of sight or wasn't seen close up or talked with people who knew him well. That's why he kept to the farm. Anyway, he'll likely throw a fit or something when he walks in at the airport tomorrow.'

'I wouldn't mind being there to see it myself,' said Nancy.

'Why not?'

'Tck!' said Nancy reprovingly. '*Somebody* has to mind the office.'

I put the phone down and told Ben. 'I'll be well enough to go with you,' he announced grimly. 'I . . . ' The doorbell rang and his head jerked.

'That'll be the doc,' I said.

It was. Dr. Jamison was a tall gangling man with piercing blue eyes and a faint whisky breath. He gave me a fast look as he came in with his faded black bag.

I said: 'I'm the fellow who called your surgery. I'm a sort of friend of Ben's.'

He gave me a hand which felt like warmed granite. 'Any friend of Ben's is a friend of mind.' He let his piercing gaze swivel to the patient. 'You look in what is usually known as a bloody mess,' he said genially.

'I'd be in a worse one but for Shand, doctor.'

'Oh — how's that? No, don't tell me yet. I'd better have a look at you first.' Jamison opened his bag and went to work. After a while he said: 'It's a type of influenza. One of the new viruses, probably imported. Not Mao 'flu, but something akin to it. That's what we get in these days of easy travel and communication. Could get worse. I'll have the ambulance sent out.'

'Now, look here, doctor . . . '

'I'll arrange it now on your phone, Ben,' said Dr. Jamison coolly.

'Dammit, I want to go to London in the morning,' roared Ben.

'What you want and what you're going

245

to do are quite different things, Ben — unless you're willing to run the risk of complications.'

'You mean it's as bad as that?'

'Well, I'm not saying you're about to die, but I'd like to have you under observation for a day or two. Got to isolate this damned bug you've collected. In any case, you can't go haring off to London because you're running a temperature.'

Ben Leffiney sighed. 'All right, you're the doctor. I suppose I can take a hot bath before the ambulance comes?'

'No harm. You look as if you need one.' Jamison grinned. 'You have the general appearance of a man who's been dragged through a hedge backwards, to coin a phrase.'

'It felt like it,' replied Ben.

'Oh, and what's that supposed to mean, or shouldn't I ask?'

Ben looked swiftly at me. I nodded and he said: 'It's a regular pippin of a story. Mr. Shand had better tell you.'

I did and at the end of it Dr. Jamison said: 'The local police should be told.'

'I'll do that, doctor, in the next few minutes. I only found Ben a short while ago.'

'Damned lucky for him you happen to be involved in all this.' Jamison glanced at the patient and added: 'So you're going to be a rich man, Ben.'

'It seems like it . . . '

'Well, don't let it go to your head.'

'No danger. It'll be a relief, though, not to have to worry about money.'

'Yes, people who say money is unimportant are either fools or they've already got plenty. Just the same, it isn't everything. And I hope you won't be living permanently in the States.'

'That's a nice speech,' said Ben.

'It was meant. You're a farmer and you belong round these parts, one of us.'

'Well, I don't know just what I'm going to do. I'll have to see.'

Jamison nodded abruptly, called the ambulance service and then the medical officer at the hospital. 'I'll be along to see you later,' he said and left.

Ben took a bath, put clean clothes on and sat in one of the faded armchairs. He had stopped shivering, but he had a flush and still looked ill.

I put a call through to Power and arranged to make a statement to the police. When I was putting the receiver down Ben said suddenly: 'I've just remembered something. That bloody swine Holburn made a funny remark today.'

'Oh?'

'Well, it seemed funny. He said something about having gone into the Leffiney ancestry and there might be another legal claimant.'

I stared. 'What — round here?'

'He didn't say that, just that there might be someone — but that even if there was he thought they'd know nothing about the fortune.'

'What claimant — I mean did he give a name?'

'No, he didn't say that, either. He just said there might be someone.'

'According to the parish records, you're the sole surviving relative, Ben.'

'So I gather, but that's what he said.'

'When was this?'

'After he came back one afternoon.'

'Came back from where?'

'He didn't say. P'raps he'd been looking things up at Somerset House.' Ben made a wry grin. 'If there *is* someone else with a legal claim bang go my dreams.'

'I've checked everything out with the rector and as far as I can see you're the man, Ben.'

'I hope so. I've had rather a bad time lately. Partly my fault, I dare say. But I had a poor harvest last season and a lot of tax to pay on the previous year, which was a good one. The trouble was I'd had to use most of the money to live on and stay in business, so I hadn't made anything like full provision for the taxman.'

'That's happened with me,' I said. 'Not lately, but I've had the experience. You just have to keep struggling.'

'I know, but I got depressed and I let things slide a bit on the farm.' He shrugged. 'Well, even if I don't come into all this easy money I dare say I'll survive. I've done it before.'

'Quit worrying, Ben. You're the heir.'

'It's a fantastic thought,' he said.

'But pleasant — it'll speed your recovery!'

'I dare say. Just now I feel shocking. My brain's like cotton wool.' His forehead puckered and he added: 'There *was* something else, I've been struggling to remember what it was . . . Holburn said that what made him think there might be another claimant was something he found at Grange Manor . . . '

'So he *was* there the night of the raid?'

'Must've been.'

'What was it he found, did he say?'

'Yes, I've got it now. It was a cameo portrait. Apparently, he shoved it in a pocket without thinking and brought it back here.'

'You mean he brought it back after the robbery — and only said there might be another claimant today?'

'Yes, I reckon so.'

'A portrait of whom?'

'He didn't say. Do you think it matters?'

'I don't know, Ben.'

He grinned wryly again. 'I certainly don't want to queer my own pitch, but p'raps we ought to find out.'

I didn't answer. A minute later the ambulance arrived. I saw him off, promised to keep in touch and started for Grange Manor.

18

The forest road was empty. Plenty of opportunity to think — but the thoughts were about as productive as a dog chasing its own tail.

I gave it up and trod on the accelerator pedal, taking the last two miles with the needle pushing hard at the seventy mark. Then I was there.

The balloon-faced butler opened the door to me. His gooseberry eyes bulged in recognition.

'Why, Mr. Shand! A pleasure to see you again. I thought you'd returned to — ah — the Metropolis, sir.'

'I had, but I've come back. Is Lady Arkwright in?'

He shook his head. 'Her Ladyship has returned to the town house in Mount Street, sir. She felt unable to stay on here alone in view of the circumstances ... ' His voice faltered.

'I understand. Do you mind if I come in for a talk?'

'Not in the slightest, sir.' He led the way to his pantry. 'Er — would you care for a drink, sir?'

'No, thanks. You go right ahead, though.'

'If you don't mind, sir, I think I will have a glass of port. I find it stimulating and — er — stimulating.'

He produced a dusty bottle and poured. The bouquet suggested something like the old '98 vintage. 'You — ah — mentioned that you wished to have a chat, sir?' he prompted.

'Yes, I'm trying to get some information and you may have it.'

'If there are any means open to me to proffer needed assistance I shall be most happy to embrace them,' he intoned. 'What precisely is it you desire to know?'

'First, has an inventory been made of all the valuables stolen from here?'

'It was put in hand immediately.'

'By whom?'

He made a small indulgent smile. 'By myself, sir.'

He coughed delicately, as might a butler caught in a mountain mist. 'If I may be permitted the observation, sir, no one — not even her Ladyship — has a deeper and more comprehensive knowledge of the objay dar of the Manor than myself.'

'That's fine, Mr. Meedes. What I'd like are details of any cameo portraits missing.'

'There was only one, sir,' said Septimus Meedes promptly. 'A .small gilt-framed portrait.'

'I guess you don't happen to know who it was of?'

'No, sir.' He eyed me curiously. 'If you will pardon the question — is it important?'

'That's what I'm trying to find out. Was the portrait of a man or a woman?'

'A woman . . . well, little more than a young girl. Perhaps seventeen or eighteen. Very beautiful she looked.'

'Some bygone member of the family?'

'No, sir, it wasn't a family heirloom or anything like that.'

'How old would it be?'

'Eighteen ninety-one approximately. I should explain that Sir James acquired it quite recently. It was one of two portraits of the same subject. But he only purchased one of them.'

I was oppressed by the feeling that nothing seemed to be leading anywhere. I tried another approach. 'Do you know if there was anything in the back of the frame, behind the actual portrait, I mean?'

'I'm sure I could not say, sir,' he said in a slightly startled tone. 'What sort of thing?'

'That's what I'm trying to find out.' I hesitated no more than a moment before telling him everything. He heard me out with just the right blend of curiosity and astonishment. Then he produced a small fruity sound; the sound of a butler chuckling. 'Some people have all the luck,' he said feelingly.

'Yeah — if there isn't a second claimant. There probably isn't. Where did Sir James buy this portrait — in London?'

'Why, no, sir. Oddly enough, he came across it at an antique shop not far from here. A small place called Diss . . . ' He broke off, staring. 'Is something wrong?'

I shook myself. It was crazy, impossibly crazy. A portrait of a young girl painted long ago, in a vanished age. What had a cameo portrait bought in a little East Anglian town to do with anybody's inheritance? But the town was called Diss . . .

I heard myself saying: 'The name of the shop, do you know it?'

'Yes, I can give it to you right away. You're sure there's nothing wrong, sir?' he asked anxiously.

'Nothing's wrong, Mr. Meedes. Everything's suddenly gone slightly mad, that's all.'

It took me twenty-five minutes to drive to Diss. The shop was just off the long street which flows past the pretty mere almost in the middle of the beautiful little town. I pushed the door open and a small man wearing a black skull-cap looked up, his pale blue eyes blinking over half-moon rimless spectacles; an old, old man with a face ruddier than the cherry.

'Yes, sir?' The voice had a slightly

sing-song intonation, but it wasn't qua-
vering, though he could be pushing
eighty.

'Mr. Jonathan?'

He nodded, beaming. I told him my
name and went on: 'I'm interested in one
of two identical cameo portraits, late
Victorian, in gilt frames, probable date of
manufacture 1891, both showing a young
woman. The late Sir James Arkwright
bought one of the pair quite recently.'

The old man eyed me curiously. 'How
do you come to know that, sir?'

'I've just come from Grange Manor,
the butler there told me.'

'Ah, I see. You are a friend of the
family, I take it?'

'Not exactly. I'm a private investigator.'

'Oh, dear,' said Mr. Jonathan. 'I hope
there is nothing amiss about these
portraits . . . '

I leaned on the worn counter and said:
'No, it's all right. I'd just like to see the
other one. I'd better explain that I'm
co-operating with the authorities in
connection with the murder and robbery
at Grange Manor. The stolen property

included the portrait in the cameo setting.'

'I see,' he answered uncertainly.

'If you'd prefer to phone County Police Headquarters I think Detective Inspector John Power will vouch for me, Mr. Jonathan.'

'Oh!' The name-dropping seemed to impress him and he added conversationally: 'Dreadful business about Sir James — dreadful.'

'Yes.'

'I hope the police apprehend the murderer, Mr. Shand.'

'They will. You haven't sold the second cameo, I hope?'

'No, sir. As a matter of fact, Sir James himself would have taken it, only the frame was chipped in several places.'

'What I'm really interested in is the history of the portrait — and, specifically, who sat it,' I said.

He twitched his glasses off his nose, polished the lens and put them back. 'There, I fear, I can't help you.'

'They must have been in the possession of a family, surely?'

'Quite so, but I don't know the name.' He smiled indulgently. 'I often acquire objects from private sellers, but not in this instance. The two cameos — and a number of other articles which I bought along with them — formed part of the sale catalogue at an auction in Norwich. It's possible that the auctioneers may know the name of the original owner, though I doubt it.'

'Oh, why?'

'The portraits were executed getting along for eighty years ago and I believe they had changed hands a number of times since then. If you think it'll help I can give you the name and address of the auctioneers, though.'

'Thanks — but if they don't know the original owner I'd be wasting my time.'

'Well, I did make some inquiries about the cameos and several other articles, but nobody seems to know their origin.'

'In that case, you won't know the identity of the sitter.'

'No, I'm afraid not. I'm sorry.'

'That's all right, Mr. Jonathan. What you don't know you can't tell me. Can I see the portrait?'

'But of course. I'll get it for you.' He was gone perhaps a minute. Then he came back and laid the cameo on an oblong faded black velvet. 'The frame, which, as you can see, is exquisitely ornamental, is partly oxidized silver but mainly what we call parcel gilt,' he said.

It was a portrait in water-colours of a young woman with her hair coiled on her head after the mode of the period. Her lips were lightly pursed, almost as if making a kiss.

I stared down at it for a long moment. Mr. Jonathan fiddled with a solid silver albert across his shiny black waistcoat. I heard him saying: 'You seem extraordinarily interested, sir . . . almost as if you were looking at someone you know.'

'Yeah,' I said thickly.

19

I phoned Linda's flat, but she wasn't there. Just the ringing tone and nobody answering. I got Nancy, though, and told her what to do. Then I drove to London. I went straight to New Scotland Yard. It was 2.27 p.m.

Logan was in his office. He listened without interruption until I had finished telling him everything — except the fantastic conjecture about the cameo portrait.

Then he said evenly: 'You think that Holburn, the fellow who's trying to gyp this man Leffiney out of his inheritance, may be on the way to Cornwall?'

'Well, he left in the real Ben Leffiney's truck.'

'That doesn't prove where he was making for.'

'No, but Borge called him at the farm.'

'I don't doubt what you say — but Holburn wasn't there to take the call.'

'I've thought of that. He must have contacted Borge or Francesco, just as he contacted my office to find out about the flight time. He wasn't at the farm, so he used a phone some place else.'

'H'm, that's probable. Yes, it's certainly probable. Just the same, I don't think your man is in Cornwall.'

I started. 'Something's happened,' I said slowly. 'Something you haven't told me.'

'That's right,' replied Logan cheerfully. 'I was coming to it, though. The Cornwall business is off.'

'What the hell do you mean it's off?'

'Exactly what I said. There isn't going to be a new art steal down there.'

'Are you going to tell me why?'

'No reason why not. Some characters who are almost certainly part of Francesco's lot have been looking at the place all right — but they've gone.'

'Why?'

Logan made an imperceptible movement with his shoulders. 'I'm not privy to their private consultations, Shand. All we know is that they've left the area.'

'Why would Francesco send guys down there for nothing?' I said. 'It doesn't figure.'

'They could've spotted the local police, though I don't think so. Second thoughts, more likely. There could be several explanations. The point is that they left.'

'You know this as a fact, you mean?'

'The squad car driver got through to Information at county police headquarters reporting that they left in a black Humber Imperial.'

'They might have gone only a few miles.'

'The police driver followed them to Truro. Then they went north on the A 3076 to Newlyn Downs and east on the A 30 — which, for your information, is the direct trunk route for London.'

'They could have turned back at some point.'

'I haven't finished yet,' said Logan impassively. 'The Humber stopped at a café and the police driver went in. He heard one of them say they were leaving — going to London.'

'And?'

'They left all right. That was when our driver phoned in — or, rather, he used the two-way radio . . . '

'Are you telling me these fellows didn't notice a police car sitting on their tail?' I asked sourly.

'No, they may well have seen it. In fact, the appearance of a police car may have had something to do with their decision to leave, though we don't think the car was noticed in the vicinity of Harbold House.'

'And?'

'The driver didn't attempt to follow them any further. It wasn't necessary if they were making for London. We've got cars out watching traffic coming in from the A 30. No luck so far, but there's time. The message came through only a short while ago. Also, we have the registration of the Humber they were using. Don't worry, we'll get them.'

'On what charge?'

'We haven't got that far, Shand. What we plan is to have them followed to wherever they're going, which is probably Francesco's place in town.'

'And then?'

'We'll have to see. Can't very well nick these chaps for what happened in Switzerland and Italy. That's a bit complicated. But if they've got some pieces of property, stolen property I mean, that would do nicely.'

'Meanwhile, you've called off the watchdogs down in Cornwall?'

'As things stand, yes. There doesn't seem to be anything to watch.'

I picked up my hat. Logan said: 'Your New York trip — that'll be off now, I take it?'

'What else?'

'This fellow Holburn,' said Logan meditatively. 'It's not our affair, in a specific sense, but if he's committed an indictable offence down in Norfolk, or any kind of offence, it's something for Power.'

'I've been in touch with him.'

'Good. I thought you would have done, anyway.'

'If Holburn shows at Heathrow in the morning he'll find the law waiting for him.'

'That's fine. But what do you mean *if* he turns up?'

'Well, if he's involved with this mob various things could happen between now and tomorrow morning,' I said.

Logan gave me a long, level look. There was no special expression in it; there wasn't anything in it that you could analyse. 'Such as what?' he said gently.

'You might have arrested him by then.' It wasn't the real answer and for a moment I thought Logan was going to take me up on it, but he didn't. Instead, he said: 'We shall want to see you later. Also Miss Travers. You'll keep in touch, naturally.'

'Naturally,' I said.

I went back to my offices in Baker Street. Nancy was looking as nearly excited as she ever looks. She came out from behind her desk with a typewritten sheet of quarto paper.

'It stands up!' she exclaimed.

'I was sure of it, Nancy.'

'Everything you said on the telephone, it checks.'

'Details?'

She nodded. 'They're all here. I went to

Somerset House and I also did some telephoning around, quite a bill you'll be getting.'

'That's all right, old man Leffiney will foot it.'

'My goodness, this whole business becomes more incredible nearly every minute,' Nancy said.

'Yeah.' I took the cameo portrait from my pocket and showed it to her. 'The girl in that painting is almost a ringer for Linda Travers,' I said.

I got the painted picture out of its chipped gilt frame and turned it over. Written on the back, in neat faded characters, were the words: *Linda Maud Travers, August, 1890, High Corners, North Walsham, Norfolk.*

'Even the given name's the same,' commented Nancy. 'Do you want to see what I've put down on paper?'

I nodded and took it from her. What she had typed was in chronological sequence and clear as crystal —

September 1, 1900: Linda Maud Delaney married to Richard James

Travers, both of Diss, Norfolk.

June 4, 1908: Daughter born and christened Janet Mary.

May 2, 1931: Janet Travers married to Robert Charles Leffiney, of Thetford, Norfolk.

December 6, 1931: Robert Leffiney changed name by deed poll to Robert Travers.

July 9, 1940: The present Linda Travers born at Highgate, London.

'Any questions?' asked Nancy.

'One — why did he change his name?'

Nancy tapped her small white teeth with her ball-point. 'I had more trouble digging *that* than all the rest put together, simply because it was so long ago. Sparing you the tedious details of my investigation, I finally discovered that he was a writer of children's books and had used his wife's name as a pseudonym — probably thought it sounded better than Leffiney. What made him adopt it as his own is something else again. I didn't find that out.'

'It may still have been what you said, he

thought it sounded better. As simple as that.' I filled a pipe and went on: 'Old man Leffiney told me he did have a younger brother named Robert with whom he had lost all contact and presumed to be dead. He thought the brother died a bachelor.'

'You'd better have another costly trans-Atlantic call and tell him to do some powerful re-thinking then, hadn't you?' Nancy said.

'Yeah — this makes Linda Travers his niece.' I blew smoke out and fanned it with my left hand. 'It also changes the inheritance set-up. Ben Leffiney is a second cousin.'

'I feel sorry for the poor man,' said Nancy. 'Having his hopes raised like that only to be dashed to the hard ground.'

'Tough luck, but it can't be helped. I'll have to call the old man — but first I want to speak with Linda.'

'Miss Travers,' said Nancy with a small emphasis on the formal description, 'hasn't been back to her apartment all day so far.'

'She's probably at the magazine's

offices. Did you try there?'

'No, it didn't seem urgent, I mean I thought it could wait as you'll be seeing her tonight, I gather.'

'I didn't tell you I was, did I?'

'I just got that impression. Well, you'll certainly brighten her life, won't you?'

I didn't answer. I was preoccupied with another thought, the one that had been with me ever since I first saw the cameo; the thought I had had while I was talking with Logan and had kept back. Now, with the knowledge that Linda was the grand-daughter of the girl in the picture and was in reality Linda Leffiney, the thought had swollen, like a darkening cloud. I remembered the way Holburn had looked at her, the sudden penetrating look which hadn't meant anything at the time. But now I *knew*. He wouldn't miss the almost uncanny resemblance — and he had told Ben there could be another claimant. Yeah, but he had said the claimant couldn't possibly know. Just the same, suppose he had checked-out the relationship? Maybe that was one reason why he hadn't been at the farm. I felt a cold grip at my stomach. But he couldn't do anything because she wasn't at her apartment, unless she came back early and . . .

Suddenly, sweat pooled down the small of my back. I almost jumped at the telephone. I called International Magazines and got the Features Editor. A woman with a faintly metallic voice.

I said: 'May I speak to Miss Linda Travers?'

'I'm sorry, but Miss Travers is out.'

'On an assignment, you mean?'

'Well . . . no.'

'Then can you tell me where she's gone?'

The voice took on a little more metallic edge. 'Who is speaking, please?'

'I'm a friend of Miss Travers, my name is Dale Shand.'

The voice made a startled sound. 'I don't understand, Mr. Shand. Miss Travers went out to meet you, at your own request, three hours ago.'

The sag at my belt felt zero cold. 'I didn't ask her to meet me,' I said.

'You — what was that you just said?'

'I haven't time to explain, just accept

271

that it is so. Where was she supposed to be meeting me?'

'In Exeter.'

I could hear my own breathing, harsh down my nose. 'How did she get this message?'

'By telephone. She didn't take the call herself, our switchboard operator passed it on. Miss Travers mentioned that it was to meet you at the airport in Exeter and that you would be there to meet the plane. She said you had uncovered a new development in connection with the articles she's writing.'

'Christ,' I said.

It didn't seem to upset her. She said levelly: 'You mean someone has decoyed her?'

'Yeah. Will you ring New Scotland Yard for me? I'll give you the name to ask for. Tell him what you've told me, and that I'm already on my way.'

'Right,' she said.

I drove to the airport and got a cancelled seat on a flight going to Exeter.

20

It was the shortest flight I had ever taken and the longest. I sat rigid in my seat like a stone man, not even smoking. I kept looking at my watch, watching countless eternities dragging by on crippled feet.

It was hot in the pressurized cabin and men were loosening ties and peeling off jackets, but I was still cold. I had known she could be in danger and I should have warned her. I *had* called her apartment — but I should have called the magazine offices earlier, before he did it. But I had thought she was safely working and that he wouldn't even try anything except at her flat, if he got the address and he would. Because she wasn't there I'd thought she was out of his reach. God Almighty, do you call that thinking, Shand? I don't know, I don't know anything except that somehow I've got to get to her before . . .

Icy sweat rolled down my back, making

a spreading lake against my shirt. A stewardess drifting down the gangway asked if I was all right. I nodded, not speaking. She hesitated, then went away.

I struggled to make my brain work, to anticipate what he would do. Suppose he took her in the truck back to Norfolk, back to the farm where he would have to kill Ben Leffiney because he thought Ben was still there, locked in the cellar?

No, it wasn't going to be like that, was it? Otherwise, why go to Exeter? He was going to St. Mawes first — his last job for Juan Francesco, the onc he couldn't side-step. He would drive to Norfolk through the night when it was all over, taking her with him. He would have just enough time because he wasn't due at Heathrow until noon. He could kill both of them and bury them or wall them up in the cellar. But he might kill her *before* that . . .

I pulled myself together, forcing myself not to weave alternatives. This was one time when that wasn't going to help. But suppose . . . shut up, Shand. For God's sake, quit thinking.

The cool, detached voice of the pretty stewardess came over the microphone: 'We are coming into Exeter. Will you please fasten your seat belts and put out your cigarettes? Captain Malleson and his crew hope you have enjoyed your flight.'

Like hell I had. I almost ran down the steps to the concrete. The private-hire car I had booked through one of the big agencies was waiting for me, but I had to pick up the keys at a small bureau in the airport building.

That took no more than minutes, but I needed every last second of them. Even in a Rover 2000 it was still quite a drive. I took the A38 through Ashburton on the southern rim of Dartmoor, missing the magnificent modern city centre they have in Plymouth, and swept out over the Tamar Bridge and on through Saltash to Liskeard. A handful of miles west of the town I made the left turn on to the A390, heading for St. Austell and Truro.

Then I was going down steep, winding roads to the King Harry Ferry which cuts about eighteen miles off the overland trek to St. Mawes by spanning the Carrick Roads.

It was 7.55 p.m. There was a line of holiday traffic waiting to get on the ferry, curling up the slope from the tiny quay. I missed one trip by a car's nose and sat there with tight hands on the steering wheel and the gear shift in first; as if that was going to make any difference.

Then I drove down on to the ferry, right up to the big gates at the front. A man came up and gave me a ticket and I got out to stretch my legs.

Away to the left a tall naval training ship was rocking at her moorings. Green-walled hills rose from each side of the sheer blue water. I stood at the head of the ferry, getting clear air into my lungs. We were half-way across when I climbed up the steps to the raised deck for a better view and, more specifically, just to have something to do other than think.

Somebody came up behind me. I could hear his footsteps tapping the narrow deck. Then they stopped. There wasn't any reason why they shouldn't, but I turned. I walked back along the deck. There was a lavatory near the top of the steps and he was standing almost behind it. He had a small black box in one hand, like a transistor radio with a mast — except that in the other hand he was holding something I couldn't clearly see and was speaking into it.

There was nobody else about, they were all sitting in their cars down below. I closed in fast and heard him saying: 'Loomis to Borge . . . are you receiving me . . . are . . . '

He saw me as I slammed the transmitter out of his hand. It sailed out, high over the rails and down into the swirl of water as the ferry rode on.

His face was a silent snarl and his right hand moved so fast that I almost didn't see the movement. Almost. I hit him just the once with everything I had. The impact sent him staggering against the rails. He hung backwards over them, fighting to regain his balance, but he was too far over. In the next moment he dropped straight down over the side.

Nobody saw it happen and I didn't yell it out loud.

Just then I didn't care if he couldn't swim. He had been going to kill me. I leaned over the side, though. Just curiosity. He could swim all right. But now he was far behind the ferry and he wasn't going to use the transmitter and he wasn't going to St. Mawes in time to do anything.

★   ★   ★

I drove off the ferry and on the last lap to St. Mawes. If there is a more beautiful little seashore resort in England I don't know where it is, but I hadn't the time to browse. I simply drove along the curving quayside with its pretty hotels and small elegant shops and on to a headland, looking for Harbold House.

It was within sight of the fairyland setting of the Church of St. Just in Roseland; set back from the narrow roadway, screened by tall privets and gently nodding trees. I drove straight past them, following the road round the plateau which formed the summit of the headland and catching a first glimpse of the fine, white-painted Georgian house picked out with dark green on its doors and window frames.

A stone wall spanned the rear of the place, flanking open double doors. Beyond the doors was a wide gravelled square. Two cars stood on it, a Rolls and a Bentley which was a ringer for the one I had seen in London.

I left the hired Rover under the shadow of the stone wall and slid round the open doors, going sideways into a small thicket of trees and only just in time. A figure emerged from the rear of the house, a man in chauffeur livery. A cigarette hung laxly from his mouth and a silenced gun was in his hand, not laxly. He stared towards the open doors, then swivelled his gaze round, but by now I was down behind massed rhododendrons.

Over his shoulder he called: 'I thought I heard a car, but it must've gone on. Everything's okay.' Then he went back into the house.

I stood up, stepped back under the

trees and picked my way through them. They ended abruptly maybe a dozen feet from the house. This would be the hazardous part because now I had no cover, even the slimmest. I waited. How long? Perhaps a full minute. The liveried man didn't come out again. Nobody came. A light breeze drifted in from the ocean and I could just hear the ceaseless fall of long breakers on the distant shore. There was no other sound. I took the automatic out, freed the safety-catch and jumped.

That took me a third of the way across the intervening space. I landed without sound on soft, yielding turf. Then the grass ended and I was on a paved walk. I went along it past wide french windows, almost doubled-up, and got to the rear door.

It opened on a lofty kitchen with red and cream fitments, a stainless steel double-drainer sink, an electric dish-washer and what looked like the biggest refrigerator in the world. There were four straight-backed chairs in the room and each one had a tenant, trussed and gagged. Two men and two girls with panic in their eyes. The same technique as before.

I hadn't time to cut them free; besides, the girls looked ready to scream. I went through a facing door and along a tiled corridor into a dim, cool hallway with doors leading off on each side. The one on my right was ajar and a remembered voice was speaking.

' . . . you are comfortable, *amigo*?' A deep chuckle, then: 'The host should always be comfortable, even a reluctant host.'

Nobody answered. Francesco went on: 'Everything has proceeded exactly as planned, after all. We load the fruits of our labours off Mullion Cove at eleven o'clock precisely and sail at 11.25, beyond all chance of pursuit. A toast, I think — with our reluctant host's admirable champagne, eh?'

Francesco laughed. Glasses clinked. Then he was speaking again. 'It was fortunate that you made that call to the farm, Borge. You still say the man who took it was Shand?'

'I cannot be certain, but so I think. I have an acute ear for voices. He tried to disguise his. That in itself arouses suspicion.'

'I am grateful for your acumen, my friend,' said Francesco.

'Holburn ought to be told . . . '

'*Si*, but I knew nothing of this development until you arrived back from the yacht only recently. However, we will inform him shortly, eh?'

'He leaves us tonight, doesn't he?'

'When he has completed his allotted task, yes. Our friend has a personal venture in hand, most ingenious.'

'So I gather,' said Borge.

'An essay in deception which delights my Machiavellian instincts. So I do not propose to hold him to his contract with us.'

'He's going back to the farm, then?'

'It is necessary, he tells me. I do not know the details, but I can guess them. He assumed the identity of another man and it is necessary to . . . dispose of him.'

'Suppose Shand is on to him?'

Francesco made another laugh. 'Should

we worry ourselves about that, *amigo*?'

'Perhaps not — but if Holburn lands in trouble of any kind he might talk to the authorities about us.'

'By which time we shall be far beyond the arm of the stupid British law, or any kind of law. We have completely outwitted them. Because of your astuteness we made a special search. Otherwise we might not have observed the police car, which was very well concealed. So we then call off the entire operation, taking care that the ridiculous police driver is made aware of this when we stop presumably on our way back to London.'

'He heard what was said all right.'

'And hastened away to inform his superiors of our assumed change of plan. So then the hunt is called off — and we simply retrace our steps after an appropriate interval and help ourselves to our host's art collection, which is beyond all doubt one of the most remarkable extant.'

Borge said: 'Just the same, I'll feel better when we're out of here, Juan.'

'Because of Shand, you mean?'

'*Ja* — he is the dangerous one. I should like . . . '

'You would like to submit him to the intricate tortures which you devised as an officer of the SS at the Gestapo headquarters in Paris, eh?'

'Those — and later techniques.'

'That was to have been the privilege of our good friend Gonzales. Alas, he failed rather signally.' Francesco sighed falsely. 'It was necessary, instead, to deal with *him*.'

Another voice. Jiri's. 'I gave him the swift exit, El Rapier. He is now among the little fishes in the Gulf of Genoa.'

'With the concrete slab neatly secured to his feet and the intestinal tract duly punctured, so that he will not float to the surface. Poor Gonzales . . . '

The door wasn't ajar enough to see. I went away, found a smaller passage going down one wall of the room. There was a door at the end, leading on to the paved walk at the other side of the house. I stepped out. The french windows were just round the gable end. By standing directly to the side of them

284

I could see into the room.

A tall man with greying hair and a tanned face was sitting in a chair with manacled hands between his knees. A long, puckered scar curved upwards from his left temple.

Francesco said: 'You are still stubborn, Mr. Glanville. That is both foolish and unrewarding, since in the final analysis you will tell us exactly what we wish to know.'

Glanville's mouth made a long, hard line. He didn't speak.

Francesco went on, musingly: 'A rare Cézanne, previously unknown and with another painting on the back, was purchased by you for two hundred and fifty thousand dollars from Julius Rotha in Amsterdam. We have so far been unable to locate it here.'

'I shall tell you nothing . . .'

Francesco smiled. 'Do not imagine, my friend, that we are to be balked of this prize. It will join many others I have acquired — the word is so much more agreeable than stolen, is it not?'

'You won't find it easy to sell them,'

said Glanville curtly.

Francesco raised surprised eyebrows. 'My dear fellow, I am not proposing to sell them. You do not believe this? Let me explain my motives. I am a collector in the truest sense — one who delights in the contemplation of created beauty. I have no thought of vulgar gain. I steal because both the planning and the hazards are a delight to me.'

'You won't get away with it, Francesco.'

'That has been said to me on other occasions, and always the speakers have been wrong. Perhaps you would care to know where your collection will finally rest, in ineffable peace and boundless if silent acclaim? I will tell you . . . my home is a medieval castle on the remotest shores of the Black Sea, an area where my every desire is anticipated and, better still, instantly obeyed.'

Francesco lit a cigar, drawing meditatively on its rolled opulence. 'Now, my dear fellow, *where is the missing Cézanne?*'

Glanville sat without movement, looking at him. There was fear in his eyes but there was courage, too. He was going to need it.

Suddenly, Francesco's urbanity fell from him like a dropped cloak. 'We have brought the means of persuasion with us, you fool,' he snarled.

Borge went across the room. When he came back he was carrying what looked like a giant's boot. He jerked one of Glanville's suede shoes off, fitted the huge boot on the stockinged foot and turned a small steel lever at the side of the instrument. Glanville's face was chalk-white under the tan, his whole body stiffened in anticipation.

'Turn it again, Borge,' ordered Francesco.

Borge made three full turns. Sweat jumped from Glanville's face in enormous globules.

The Spaniard took the cigar from his mouth and studied it. Without looking up he said: 'Break some of the bone structure . . .'

I shot glass out of one of the panes in the french windows and went back the way I had come, back along the slim passage and into the wide hallway. I kicked the door right in.

They were crowded round the windows, four of them — Francesco, Borge, Jiri and the uniformed chauffeur. Borge heard me and started a fast turn, but before he could make it I shot him below the right kneecap. He banged down on the carpet, yelping. He wasn't going to get up again in a hurry.

I said tightly: 'Keep the hands out where I can see them, *amigos*.'

Only Francesco looked unperturbed. The big bland smile was still in position, false as all getout, but it was there. 'Mr. Shand — how amiable of you to drop in on our little gathering.'

'The joke's over, Mr. Rapier.'

'Ah, but for whom? As the English say, the game is never won until it is lost.'

Borge was crawling sideways, dragging his leg, like a mosquito with a torn wing. He clawed at his dropped gun. I ground a heel down on his hand and kicked the automatic skittering into a corner.

'Take that boot off Glanville, one of you,' I said.

The chauffeur did it. Then he stood

there with the thing, his body half-bent and hunched forward, evil eyes glaring from his ratty face.

Glanville whispered: 'Who . . . who are you?'

'A friend — I'll tell you everything later.' I looked at them. 'Put your guns on the floor — also knives.'

Jiri said: 'Drop dead, bastard!'

'Do as he asks, Jiri,' said Francesco. 'You, too, Maxie.'

Two Smith and Wesson thirty-eights, a nine-shell Luger and two knives with ornamental handles. Francesco said musingly: 'You would not, perhaps, be interested in a business proposition, Mr. Shand?'

'Proposition me.'

'You are a man of infinite resource and perseverance with a flair for eluding defeat. Such qualities are most rare. It occurs to me that you might possibly care to join our little band of *entrepreneurs*.'

'On what terms?'

'Admirable ones, my dear Shand. I am an immensely rich man and will pay whatever price you name.'

He said it without looking at me. I had a sudden prickly sensation down my spine. He was looking beyond me, towards the door.

There was no small current of air, no small sound, no anything. But someone was in the room . . . behind me.

21

Francesco was laughing, a soft bubbling laugh. Something hard pressed into the small of my back and went away.

'You arrive delightfully on cue, Carmen,' Francesco murmured. 'Our good friend Shand failed to take into account that you might be somewhere on the premises.'

I hadn't, but I had had to act before they fractured Glanville's foot. And now she was behind me with a gun and the joke was on me and it wasn't going to give me any kind of laugh.

From the floor Borge screeched: 'I kill him, but slowly.'

The chauffeur ran a furred tongue across his mouth. 'Let me do it,' he whispered.

'We're running out of time — kill him now,' Jiri said.

He reached down for one of the guns. His fingers were closing on the grip when Carmen said: 'Drop it, Jiri!'

'I'm giving it to him . . . '

'You didn't hear me, I said to drop it and I'm a lady who likes her own way.'

Jiri stared up, leering. His hand moved again. There was a dull hard plop. The .38 spun from his fingers, smashing into the glass of the bookcase along one of the walls. He stood where he was, his eyes disbelieving, his jaw hanging slack.

Carmen moved sideways, coming level with me. 'Hello, Shand,' she said. 'Between us we've got this little meeting called to order.'

Something not quite sane glared from Francesco's eyes. 'You . . . you are in league with Shand?'

'Not yet, but I think we can set up a deal. Two heads are better than one and I like the look of Shand as a partner.'

Francesco said in a cold deadly voice: 'What exactly are you planning, my sweet?'

She straddled her long legs, the gun rock-firm in her slim hand. 'I'm hijacking your loot,' she said calmly. 'Holburn has loaded it in his truck. He arrived half an hour ago and I watched him do it . . . '

I heard myself saying: 'You mean you looked inside?'

'No — why?'

'He's got a girl in it, the same girl Francesco's mob kidnapped. He means to kill her.'

'How do you know?'

'He's got her,' I said.

'You don't *know* that,' she said. 'Anyway, he's gone . . . '

I made a small movement. Carmen said coolly: 'Not yet, Shand. Don't worry — we'll both get after him in a few minutes.'

Without turning my head I said: 'I take it you're the one the police call The Charmer?'

'So I've heard. Nobody knows my real name, which certainly isn't Carmen. That makes things sort of difficult for the authorities. Look — Holburn's making for Mullion Cove. It's a fairish drive but we'll overtake him. Two of us is just right. Hijacking the stuff by myself was beginning to look a little dicey — too many of the enemy. Together it'll be easy. Besides, you've already done the spade-work.'

'And you want me to team-up with you?'

'Why not? I liked the way you handled things on the yacht. You're my kind of man.'

'Thanks,' I said drily. 'And then?'

'What I said — we decamp with the spoils. I know how and where to do the selling.'

'Why cut me in?'

'I need a partner. I've needed one for some time, but I never met anyone who looked like filling the bill. You do. The chances are I'd never get away with the stuff without help and I know it. Together we've got it made. I've seen you in action and that'll do nicely. Now — truss these comedians up and we'll be on our way.'

'And?'

'We cosh Holburn and drive his truck in a new direction. I'll tell you where — later.'

Suddenly, the Spaniard's voice blared, out of control. The schooled urbanity was gone, the face aged and ravaged. 'You bloody bitch, I'll hand you over to Borge and watch you die by inches . . . '

She laughed at him. 'Chance is a fine thing, Juan — only you aren't going to get even the ghost of a chance.'

Francesco swallowed convulsively. 'Fifty thousand in sterling,' he said. 'Is that enough?'

'You must be joking. The loot is worth a king's ransom. And if you doubled the money I'd never collect — not from you and not after *this*!'

'I'll kill you, with my own hands I'll kill you,' he screamed.

'You'll never find me. By tomorrow I won't even be in the country.' She used her free hand to move fingertips down the side of my face. 'We won't be in the country. A new partnership. You'll make a nice sleeping partner . . . in the literal sense, I mean.'

I said: 'No dice, Carmen — about that or the other thing.'

For a long moment she stood there, not speaking. I knew what she was going to do because there wasn't anything else. I hoped I had timed it right. I hooked a foot out from my side, round her ankle, before she could use her gun. She staggered, losing balance — then suddenly cannoned inwards against me.

Francesco lunged across the floor, going down for the Luger. I flung her off me, turned my own gun and brought it down with a crunch on his neck. He grunted and spreadeagled with his face in the carpet. In the same instant, Jiri and Maxie started a rush. I wheeled at an almost impossible angle, turning the gun back and on them.

From the door Carmen said: 'You're a bloody fool, Shand. Good-bye . . . '

There was a small click as the key snapped round in the lock. I couldn't go after her. I had to stand there covering all three. Nobody could do anything. A car motor coughed, then hummed into powered smoothness and was gone.

Francesco heaved himself up from the floor on his hands, collapsed and tried again. This time he got on his feet, swaying. The madness was still in his eyes, but he was beyond speech.

I darted a glance sideways. There was another door. I walked backwards to it and got it open.

'Inside — all of you,' I snarled.

They went in, Borge still crawling, and I banged the door on them. There was no key. I wedged a heavy chair under the trigger handle and went out through the french windows as tyres slapped the tarmac drive.

I stepped out from the gable end and there were four cars jammed with coppers, plainclothed and uniformed branch. Logan was the first out.

'I thought you'd come,' I said.

He grinned faintly. 'We worked out what was likely to be in their minds and deduced that they'd come back. Had an idea you'd do the same, only we were giving them a little time and so you got here first.'

'You were nearly too late,' I said. I explained what had happened.

Glanville came through the front entrance, one foot still without a shoe.

I added: 'The art collection has already gone . . .'

'What do you mean, gone?' barked Logan. It was the first time I had heard him raise his voice.

'Holburn loaded it on a truck. He's on

his way to Mullion Cove. Francesco has another yacht standing offshore.' I started moving away.

Logan shot out a hand. 'Where do you think *you're* going?'

'After him.'

'This is police business, Shand.'

I tore my arm free. 'He's got Linda Travers in the truck,' I said and ran for it.

I was in the Rover 2000 and gunning through the gears before they could stop me, though it was close. I didn't make for the Carrick Roads; it was no use now, the last ferry of the day had gone. I had to take the overland route through to Truro. After that the A39 and on through Long Downs to Helston. No straight roads and no dual carriageways, but I still drove fast, up to the limit of safety — and sometimes beyond.

It was nearly dark. There was no sign of the truck. But headlights swept in through the rear window, bouncing off the driving mirror. I didn't have to guess whose lights. They would be from one of the police cars.

A little more time passed, then I was

going down the last section before Helston with the law still on my tail. I cut out to pass a white Triumph Spitfire. The hood was down and her hair was streaming out in the rushing air. Carmen. I went past on a new surge of acceleration. The squad car roared in behind.

When I looked in the mirror she was turning the sports car in a wide, swinging arc, heading the other way. Maybe the law would catch-up with her later, maybe not. I almost hoped not. I owed her something, or did I?

I swung left at the big junction just short of Helston and hit the first wide stretch of road, past the naval air training base. Goonhilly Downs lay just ahead, but I wasn't going satellite spotting. I went down a steep wooded slope, up the other side and drove into the 'B' road for Mullion with the police still in step behind.

Two miles to go. Then I saw it, its bulk looming in the headlight glare. A truck. We went down the main one-way street and into the empty village.

Suddenly and without warning, he spun the truck into a tight right-hand turn. I crash-braked, going down through the gears and swerving after him on what felt like two wheels. The police car shot straight on with a crescendo squeal from tortured brakes. There was a juddering impact, the crackle of flying glass.

I was half-way down the short street, level with the parking lot of an inn, when the truck reached the bottom and turned again, going left. Now it *had* to be him. There was no other reason for what he was doing; he had seen me. Maybe not close enough to know who was following him, but enough to know he was being followed.

The road dipped steeply, then climbed. He steered madly off it, going for the rising mass of Poldhu Point, revving hard in second. He stopped on the summit. The Rover's headlights lit the whole scene up.

He was dragging her out of the truck. Then he had her in front of him, her wrists lashed behind her. His free hand held a National Match Colt, big as a cannon.

I got out, walking towards them. He saw me.

'*Shand!*' The word frothed on his mouth.

I was holding my own gun down against my right thigh. I couldn't use it. I couldn't do anything except walk.

'Don't come closer, Shand . . . ' His voice was barely audible.

He went back half a dozen paces, still dragging her, like a shield. A laugh broke from him, only half-crazed. The other half held the note of triumph.

'I don't know how you got on to me,' he said, 'but it doesn't matter now, does it?'

'No, only one thing matters . . . '

His mouth made a small twist. Nothing else happened on his face.

'Tell me,' he said.

'It's just that you're not flying to New York tomorrow to inherit the Leffiney fortune, Holburn,'

He grinned. 'I am, you know . . . don't *move*, I said.'

I stayed where he had told me, looking for a chance, any kind of chance. The squad car must have hit a shop front. It could be ten minutes before they found us and he wasn't going to give me five of them.

'I'm going to New York all right, Shand,' he said cosily. 'Only I'm going without you. I don't need you any more. I don't even need the proof because you've already provided it for old Leffiney.'

'So all you have to do is walk in, announce that you're Ben Leffiney, mention that I met with a fatal accident and collect when the old man dies.'

'That's right.' A flicker came and went in his eyes. 'Maybe he isn't going to live much longer.'

'Arsenic and old age, something like that?'

'You're getting warm, Shand.'

'It's too complicated,' I said. 'You've got to kill Ben first, as a starter.'

'I should've done it before, but it wasn't necessary until I knew for sure that I could make a real claim. Then I had to do this job. But don't worry, Shand, I'll fix everything.'

'It's still too complicated, Holburn.'

'No, it's easy. I kill you and the girl first — just like that. Then I'm in the clear. Driving away. No eyewitnesses, no anybody. Just me driving back to Norfolk and catching the plane tomorrow.'

Linda's eyes were directly on me, almost as if she were trying to convey something. I didn't know what it was. All I knew was that I had to get to her. But I couldn't move. Only talk was left, and not much of that.

'What about the loot?' I said.

He laughed. 'I've done all I'm doing. If they find the truck they can drive it down to the cove their bloody selves. There's a motor launch waiting to take the stuff to the yacht.'

'Why didn't you go there? You could have got away on the launch.'

'You're talking crap and you know it. You were too close for that. I had to think of something. It's better up here . . .'

He went back, almost to the edge of the Point. He put the gun against her neck. She made a small indescribable cry, sagging down him.

Twenty feet between us. I jumped half

the distance, hit the ground and stumbled, rolling over. He let her go and swivelled the gun round, aiming. I rolled over and over as he squeezed the trigger. The bullet tore into the ground, sending up tiny spurts of brown earth.

But the roll had taken me out of the headlights' arc. I came up fast on my feet and dived headlong for his legs before he could see to fire a second time.

We went down together. No words and no quarter. Every dirty trick in the book and some I hadn't realized I knew. I moved my body as his knee drove up, but the impact was still excruciating.

Then we were upright, locked together, swaying almost on the brink. He had a splayed-out hand clawing at my face, forcing my entire head back. I sank a short punch into his solar plexus. Breath gushed from him and the appalling pressure on my neck stopped.

I went for him with both hands. He danced sideways, his face a glaring white mask. A small tufted hummock tripped his right foot and he reeled back, both arms upflung.

For a moment he seemed to be poised, leaning far out with the upper part of his body bent the wrong way. Then he plunged straight over the edge.

He screamed.

The high keening note of it was still eddying upwards from the black rocks below as Logan ran towards me.

22

I flew to New York with Linda Travers. I'd
have taken Ben along, except that he was
still in hospital surrounded by doctors
trying to figure which bug had bitten him.

It was three in the afternoon when we
came in at Kennedy Airport. Twenty
minutes later a taxi was speeding us down
the Van Wyck Expressway.

Linda said: 'I'm scared.'

I grinned. 'Of being an heiress?'

'No it's not that. I'm scared of meeting
Mr. Leffiney.'

'Why?'

'I don't know. There isn't any reason,
but I am.'

'My information is that he's a sort of
survival from another age, but that
doesn't necessarily make him frightening.'

'No, I suppose not. I dare say I'm just
being silly.'

'I've only spoken to him on the
telephone, but I'd say you're going to like

him. The era he's outlived wasn't all that intimidating. Better than this one, in some ways, come to think of it.'

'If you had money, yes.'

'I guess that's true, though it isn't the whole story. It wasn't bad all the time and a lot of people managed to live happily in it.'

'Well, they didn't have world wars and I dare say that helped.'

'And no mass communications system, so that a fellow could live an ordered life and assume that everything was the same for everybody.'

'Not quite that, surely?'

'You mean wars were happening even then? Sure, but they weren't happening to him and he didn't have to see it on television.' I grinned again. 'Anyway, all that's nothing to do with your meeting old Jesse Melford Leffiney. Another thing — he may have outlived his era, but he'll probably start a new one when he sees you.'

She snuggled into my shoulder and folded a hand on mine. 'I like being with you, Dale — you have a way of making everything seem all right.' A small shudder rippled through her. 'But for you I don't like to think what . . . '

'Then don't, Linda. It's finished and nothing else is going to happen to you, except the pleasant things.' I glanced out of the window. We were crossing the Williamsburg Bridge. Out of sight on the East River a ship's siren wailed, a long plaintive note like a held twelve-bar phrase from the blues. Then we were on the rocky island the Dutch bought off the Red Indians for twenty dollars all those centuries ago.

Jesse Melford Leffiney was waiting for us in the house on East 72nd Street almost within sight of the Cornell Medical College. He was tall and angular and if he lived another decade he would be a hundred, but his eyes and movements were alert and he was wearing a slim single-breasted suit cut from grey banker's cloth and styled by a master craftsman of the late 20th Century. His hair, thick and gleaming like old silver, clustered in small waves above the buttoned-down collar of a white shirt offset by a navy blue silk tie with a single pearl somewhere just below dead centre.

He took both her hands and looked at her, a long appraising look. She wasn't scared now, so that he was seeing her the right way, all the beauty and calmness and the basic simplicity of her.

Then he turned to me and said quietly: 'Thank you, Shand. Thank you for finding her — and saving her.'

'She helped, Mr. Leffiney. She put on a simulated faint and that gave me my chance.'

'So you told me over the Atlantic phone, but I shall want to hear it all again. We owe you more than we can ever hope to repay.' A smile lived momentarily on his firm mouth. 'Just the same, I shall treble the bonus I contracted to pay you. I hope you will not find it ethically impossible to accept.'

'From where I'm standing ethics seem a bit shadowy, Mr. Leffiney. I guess they have a way of dissolving in the company of fifteen grand.'

We sat in the vast lounge with brilliant, inexorable sunlight pouring into the room like a solid wedge. The old man said: 'Tell me everything about yourself, my dear.'

She sat with her hands in her lap, talking quietly except when some remembered incident quickened her voice. She half-turned towards me and put out a hand. 'But for Dale I should never have known my real identity. Father never told me.'

He passed a hand over his silver hair. 'We didn't correspond other than a few desultory letters and then they ceased. Our temperaments were different. Then, of course, I was so much older and had lived all my life three thousand miles away and he left America in his teens and never came back. And now . . . ' Another smile, then: 'You will be a very rich young woman . . . '

For a moment Linda hesitated. Then she said: 'Uncle Jesse — I don't want you to leave it all to me. I'd like to share it with Ben.'

He looked at her from hazel eyes bright as a bird's. He stood up, walked to where she sat and dropped hands on her shoulders. 'I'm glad,' he said. 'I don't want to cut him out. I haven't yet had the pleasure of meeting him, but Shand likes him and I guess that's more than enough.'

The old man sat down again and added: 'Two-thirds to you as a major claimant and a third to Ben — I judge that to be equitable.' He made a dry chuckle. 'I could, of course, put that in the new will I am having drawn up, but I like it better coming from you . . . '

★ ★ ★

I had kept on my apartment in the quiet old midtown square. It was much later when we went there.

Linda said: 'It has that funny, faint kind of atmosphere — you know, the way a place gets when it's not been lived in lately.'

'The atmosphere usually reeks of tobacco smoke and solitary male occupancy.'

'Solitary?'

'Yeah.'

'You mean you've never brought a girl here before?'

'Once.'

'Oh . . . '

'I didn't sleep with her. She was tuckered-out after a pretty tough experience.'

'Like the one I had?'

'Not quite like that. She'd had a bad time, though.'

She looked directly at me and said: 'The girl in the cameo picture, my grandmother . . . '

'Yes?'

'She gave you a really gilded kiss, didn't she?'

'I guess she did, come to think of it.'

'I'll give you a better one,' Linda said. She came towards me with both arms out. I held her tightly, aware of her warm body against mine, aware of the sudden leaping within me.

After a time she took her mouth away and said: 'Are you going to sleep with me?'

I picked her up and walked across the room to the other room.

'Try and stop me,' I said.